8/2020

To my dear friend Estie,
thank you for all your
love and Kindness
Much Love,
Ruthie

Justice

Freedom Fairway

D1707241

This book is dedicated

to all of the kids that long for justice

but realize that true justice only

comes from God.

Prologue

The basketball court behind my home doesn't seem like the stage for a disturbingly sinister and ominous event. Especially since it has shiny new cement, tenderly nurtured flowerbeds, and sparkling black metal benches and trash cans.

But it *was* the stage.

Believe me. I was there.

Here's the story.

Investigations by Scout Williams: Book 1

CHAPTER 1 *The Jetson Boys*

I pedal my green mountain bike down the street, the open garage of my home in sight. Biking home from school sure is a workout.

I live in a nice neighborhood. My house is not extravagantly huge, but not mousy and small either. The ceilings are high, the clay light fixtures handmade, the countertops made of shiny, bronzy copper that dulls every time acidic citric juice is spilled on it. Near the sink, oxidation develops. The outside is charming, paneled with orangy wood. The garage is plated with a sheet of corrugated metal. The roof slopes up from the back, and our yard is lushy green with the occasional brown swelter.

As soon as I shut the white garage door that leads into the house, I walk through the hallway, which opens up to the large, open living room, dining room, and kitchen. Once I emerge from the hall, the kitchen is just to my left, the dining area to my right, and the living room beyond. Mom calls from the kitchen, "Scout?"

"Yes, Mom?"

Investigations by Scout Williams: Book 1

"I just prepared your favorite snack!" (I LOVE chocolate-dipped Doritos, I know, I'm weird). "I'm thinking no TV this afternoon. It's so beautiful out..." Mom says, getting that faraway look in her eyes. It seems every time Mom declares "no TV today" she gets that look. She slides the paper towel over the bar counter toward me.

I can't argue. This May day *is* perfect. It's *finally* starting to warm up. Today is sixty-eight degrees, sunny with a soft breeze. "Okay," I shrug, then plunge into my school backpack and retrieve my black notebook. I take it everywhere. I grab my snack and head to the back porch. I collapse in a cushioned lawn chair, bask in the welcoming sun, soaking in the inspiring scenery.

My backyard slopes down to a small valley, where the basketball court, frequently called "The Court," stands. Beyond that, the ground inclines up to the Jetsons' spacious backyard and modern mansion. The Teton mountains rise above Falcon Lake just a few miles away.

Ah, Falcon Lake. It seems to be made of pure emerald, beautifully cut. It glitters serenely like newly fallen snow, at least when the sun hits it. In overcast weather, though, the lake is different. It seems like a child of the sea, forest greens and French greys and stormy blues swirling in its foamy waters and stretching to the lake's shores. In those occasions it seems to eat the silty, stony, rocky, Idaho sand entirely, gnawing on the edges of the boardwalk constructed five feet from where the waterline usually is in calm weather.

Anyway, enough about the scenery. I should probably let you know a little bit about myself. My name is Scout Truth Williams. I'm fourteen, and my birthday is January 1. I have brown hair and

Investigations by Scout Williams: Book 1

bangs, dark brown eyes, and freckles dotted across my face. Today I'm wearing shorts, an Under Armour shirt, and scuffed sneakers.

I notice that the Jetson boys are playing basketball down at The Court. I decide to say hi. My notebook under my arm, I head cautiously down the steep hill and to the edge of The Court. Eleven-year-old Grant jogs up to me, mopping his glistening brow with a bright white towel.

Grant is about a head shorter than me. He has a standard hair cut with a long swoosh of hair pushed to the side. That swoosh always tickles his eyeballs, and Grant has to toss his head or blow wildly to keep it out of his face. He has blue eyes and large freckles around his nose. Today, he's wearing a Nike shirt with matching basketball shorts. "Hey, Scout," he gasps.

"Hi, Grant," I reply, keeping my eyes on the game. There are only boys in the Jetson family, which is fine with me because sometimes boys are more fun to hang out with than girls. They're each named after a U.S. President because their dad's a U.S. history fanatic.

Jefferson is fourteen, and he's my favorite. He has cool hair. It's dirty-blonde and short on the sides, long and curly on the top. His foggy blue eyes are insightful, and he always wears athletic clothes. Always. It's like his heart beats Nike, Adidas, The North Face, and Puma.

Last on The Court is Lincoln. His curly dark hair rolls and roils on his head, somehow gathering in the front and looking effortlessly good. (Isn't that how it always is with boys?) Lincoln is pale-skinned, with freckles crawling up his arms and sticking in the randomest places. Dead center of the index finger knuckle. Second fold of the cagina. Underneath his pinky fingernail. Lincoln has long legs—perfect for dunking—and he takes advantage of this fact.

Jefferson and Lincoln hover over each other in fierce competition. Jefferson grasps the basketball, pivoting on one foot, while Lincoln swats at it. "Who's winning?" I ask Grant.

"It's a tie right now… Jefferson thinks he can make that shot…Ooh! Nice try!" Grant calls out, watching his brothers play. He looks relieved that he isn't in the pickle that Jefferson is in—having to choose whether to make a drive for the basket or shoot from his precarious position. Jefferson hook shots the ball from the half-court line, and it rolls lazily around the rim before turning to the side straight into Lincoln's waiting hands. He dribbles it to the other basket with perfect form and makes the shot with a *swish* sound.

Jefferson forces a clenched smile and slaps his forehead. Lincoln just shakes his head and laughs.

"We've never beat Lincoln!" Grant tells me like he does every time I show up on The Court. Then his eyes light up like he has just conjured up the best idea in the universe. "Hey! You wanna play? It'll make even teams…"

"Sure," I answer, hoping they would ask me.

Jefferson and Lincoln walk over. They look like lions, stalking in after the hunt. Jefferson drains a whole bottle of Gatorade in one gulp, and he leans so far back that it's a wonder he doesn't tip over. Lincoln raises his eyebrows at me, but it isn't the I'm-better-than-you look. He's smiling politely. "You playing?"

"I guess, although I'm not that good."

Investigations by Scout Williams: Book 1

Jefferson finishes the drink, twists the bottle, and tosses it into the gleaming trash can. Grant moves to join Lincoln's team. I guess he's afraid of losing. I'm stuck with Jefferson, but I don't mind. At all. "Why don't you just get Washington to play?" I question, a little uneasy that I'll fail miserably.

Washington is their oldest brother, he's eighteen and likes to read sci-fi novels. Likes to sit in a huge red beanbag chair in his room and eat stale fries from Chick-fil-A.

Jefferson rolls his neck in some kind of stretch. "He doesn't have a thing for sports."

I gulp—Jefferson's intimidating. The game starts when Lincoln checks the ball to me. Jefferson's on top of Grant like lint on clothes, and Lincoln's eyes dart from me to them. Suddenly, he starts dribbling the ball and mauls toward the basket opposite him. I follow on his heels and smash at the ball in his hands. The tall teenager is ahead of me, though. He jukes me, then jumps and releases the ball. It rolls off his long fingers perfectly. It glides into the basket without bothering to touch the rim. Lincoln runs a hand through his black curly hair and smiles.

The rest of the game goes much the same, me more of an obstacle than a help. Lincoln and Grant win.

Jefferson hi-fives me after the game and grabs another Gatorade. "You're pretty good I guess. Hey, Scout, did you hear?"

"About what?" I rub my arm.

"The kidnapping!"

"No..." I cock my head.

Investigations by Scout Williams: Book 1

"Well, there was this kid, and he got nabbed right after he—" Jefferson stops mid-sentence.

A door slams. "Boys?" A woman shouts. "Time for family work-outs!"

"Coming, Mom!" Lincoln tucks the basketball under his arm and waves his brothers to come. Mrs. Jetson was an Olympic biker and won the silver medal in cycling. She has short greying hair and a very muscular body. *Very* muscular. So muscly that I can see her muscles from here. She also home-schools her kids.

Jefferson grabs his sports bag and waves to me. I wave back, and they trudge up their hill while I trot up mine.

Jefferson's words resound in my mind. *'Nabbed...'*

CHAPTER 2 *Just Curious*

I burst through my back door, and the AC feels good. Dad sits in his large armchair, still wearing his suit and tie. He works at Williams & Sons Title Company, whatever that means. Why did he, whenever he named the company, have to add 'Sons'? The only son he has is Smith, and my brother doesn't strike me as a title company worker. Maybe more of a high school track star.

Anyway, Dad has a balding head surrounded by straight silver-streaked black hair. He's stocky with a broad chest. He's reading *The AspenVale Post*. Across the main page are the words *Child Mysteriously Missing in 'Waterways,' Neighborhood of Aspenvale, Idaho.*

The kidnapping that Jefferson was talking about. Waterways is our neighborhood. Dad speaks without taking his eyes off the paper. "Police called."

"They did?" I blurt. "What did they want?" Police officers intrigue me.

Investigations by Scout Williams: Book 1

"Wondered if we saw anything suspicious at The Court yesterday."

"Like what?"

"Questionable strangers. Creepy vans. The like."

"No, I didn't see anything," I reply, sorry I can't be involved in the action. "I was at Jennifer's yesterday."

"Mm."

Suddenly I get a brilliant idea. "Dad?"

He looks at me over the top of his small square glasses. Slightly frustrated. Slightly interested. "Mm?"

"Can you take me to the police office?"

Dad purses his lips, eyes back on the paper. "Police office?" he mumbles, saturated in the weather forecast. "Why?"

"I want to talk to the police."

"Oh?" Dad finally looks up. "About what—"

Dlling! Dliiing! Dlling! Dliiing!

Dad jumps up, fishing his phone out of his pocket. "Oh, it's the print shop," he mutters. "How could I forget...Hello, this is Roger Williams with Williams & Sons Title Company. Oh yes, Clarence, I ordered—" That's all I hear, as Dad hurries into his study and shuts the door firmly.

I sigh, watching the aspens in the backyard quiver in the breeze. They look careful yet reckless. *Now* how am I going to get info about the kidnapping Jefferson had mentioned?

Investigations by Scout Williams: Book 1

All of a sudden, the front door lurches open, letting in a gust of wind that blows the flowers in Mom's vase to the ground, spilling all the water. My sixteen-year-old brother Smith blusters in, swinging his backpack and throwing his shoes off at high speed. "Wow," I spin around. "What's the hurry?"

My brother slides across the kitchen floor in his socks, his hat falling off in the meantime. He jolts open the fridge before answering, "Mom said I could play 30 minutes of War Zone!" He studies the contents of the fridge with a humorously concentrated look before snatching a Dr. Pepper from the shelf.

"Smith, do you know anything about that kidnapping in the news?"

"Nope." My brother, in his haste, almost chokes on his soda.

"Well could you drive me to the police office?" I beg.

"No," my brother splutters, giving me a warning look for hindering his War Zone haze. He turns on the TV and grabs his controller.

"Well I need *someone* to help me," I give Smith the puppy dog eyes.

He raises his eyebrows and sighs. The controller sags in his hands. He mutters the answer he always gives when he wants me to go away. "Go talk to Jefferson."

Investigations by Scout Williams: Book 1

CHAPTER 3   *Jefferson's Explanation*

With that, I throw on my tennis shoes and trot through the backyard down to The Court. I trudge up the Jetson's backyard to their spacious back porch. It's an understanding between our two families that if we need anything, we just bang on each other's back doors. I do exactly that.

The Jetson house is enormous. There are smooth wood floors, a spiral staircase, and spasmatic, modern light fixtures. The walls are bleach white.

Grant comes panting to let me in, dripping gallons of sweat. "Yeah?" he wheezes. "What d'you want?"

"Can I talk to Jefferson?" I plead.

"Huh," he huffs, hardly listening. He leans his perspiring head on the white wall. "I guess, but you'll have to go get him." Grant's shoulder sags to the wall. "I'm dying," he mutters. "50 pull-ups and 25 push-ups are no joke. And that's not even all of it!"

Investigations by Scout Williams: Book 1

I laugh to myself. "Where's the workout room?" I call to Grant from my position near the coffee table.

The boy—still gasping his lungs out—forgets his quote-on-quote "I'm dying" and staggers into the next room to get his brother.

Jefferson bursts into the living room the same way his brother did. He lurches to the wall, inhaling and exhaling gale-force winds and clutching his sweaty side. His head tie is soaking, muscle shirt drenched, and every time his bare feet hit the floor, they squeak like Hyperdunks on a basketball court. "Huhhhh," he sighs, flopping onto the couch like a fish. "What is it, Scout?"

"Um," I try not to laugh at his drama. "Tell me about the kidnapping you were talking about earlier."

"Oh yeah," he pants. He sits up, still clutching his side. "You know Walt Johnson , right? He lives a few doors down?"

"Yeah," I reply. "Isn't he that sixth-grader who's always shooting hoops down at The Court? He's usually wearing jeans?"

"That's him," answers Jefferson. "He was playing down there yesterday or something when he just disappeared. He wouldn't answer his phone—"

"He has a phone?"

"Yeah—a flip phone."

"Ah, I see. Go on."

"Well, I heard Mom and Dad saying there's been a suspicious white van hanging around in The Court's parking lot—Dad's seen it himself." Jefferson peels his head tie off and stretches

Investigations by Scout Williams: Book 1

it out like a rubber band. "He didn't know it was owned by criminals when he saw it though—just thought it was a neighbor's car or something."

"Maybe Walt got lost or something like that...Or he could've ran away. Maybe he wasn't kidnapped," I muse.

"I guess," Jefferson shrugs. "But the police found a random mask sitting in the middle of The Court."

"A mask?" I perk up.

"Yeah," he rubs his cheek on his shoulder.

"Oh, what did it look like?" I realize I'm biting the inside of my lip. A mask. Creepy.

"Don't know for sure," Jefferson answers with another shrug. "I heard it looked like Spiderman's or something."

"Oh," I say again. I head for the door. "Thanks for the info, Jefferson."

"Yeah," he twiddles his fingers like he's searching for the right words. "But Scout," an amused look crosses his face. "Since when have you been so interested in detective stuff?"

"Don't know." Now it's my turn to shrug. "I just want justice I guess. I can't stand when people hurt someone else and don't get what they deserve. " I slip out the glass back door, ready to saddle my bike and ask some more questions.

CHAPTER 4   *What Happened to Walt*

I fasten my black helmet over my thick braid and jump on my bike. I've played with the kidnapped kid, Walt, before and I recall he lives a fourth of the way around the loop circling The Court. I swerve right out of my driveway and pedal by four well-kept houses before I park next to the curb and take off my helmet. Two police cars are parked in the driveway, and an officer in the passenger seat watches me bound to the covered brick entryway. I knock on the white front door.

While I wait for an answer, I inspect the place. There's a cute old-fashioned outdoor light bolted next to the door, and the doormat has a cartoon cacti print on it in fading colors. The house is brick, the yard is nice and plushy green. I turn to face the door once I hear loud footsteps and the unbolting of a heavy-duty lock.

Standing inside is a tall, thin lady wearing black heels, spotless white pants, and a striped-black-and-white shirt. *Does she wear these kinds of clothes every day?* I wonder. Her green eyes are attractive and her bobbed brown hair is straight and shiny. I can tell she is extremely worried even though she smiles thinly at me with small white teeth. This is Mrs. Johnson, the kidnapped kid's mother. "It's Scout, isn't it? Scout Williams?" she asks.

"Yes, ma'am," I smile back. An artificial smile. A door-to-door salesman smile. Behind her two policemen pace and a tall man in a black suit stares at me over dark tinted sunglasses.

Mrs. Johnson hesitates a second before inviting, "Won't you come in?"

I step inside. The décor is charming. The mantel is white, straddling a brick fireplace. Framed sayings like 'Home is Where the Heart Is,' and 'A Family Defines Love,' decorate the white walls, and little succulent plants dot the room. "Scout," Mrs. Johnson says. "This is Fox Ware." She gestures to the sunglasses man. "He's with the FBI."

Mr. Ware nods curtly. "I was sent here by the President himself," he announces, fingering his chin. "We are trying to crack down on these child abduction cases. They are becoming alarmingly common in our country. If you are not needed here, Scout Williams," he looks directly at me. "Please leave."

"I'm just trying to help," I plead respectfully. "Could I ask Mrs. Johnson some questions?" I propose to the intimidating man.

"I don't see the harm," replies Mr. Ware. "Just keep everything you hear to yourself."

"Well," I start, not for sure how Mrs. Johnson will respond to the question I'm about to ask. Will she cry? Will she curl up in an imaginary shell and not speak a word? Will she chase me out of the house, shouting all the while? "Um, I was wondering if you know anything about your son—"

Investigations by Scout Williams: Book 1

"Walter?"

"Yeah, Walter. I was wondering if you know anything about *Walter's* kidnapping."

She grimaces, takes a deep breath, lets it out, and laces her hands together. I notice she darts a quick glance at the amused police. "I really don't know what happened. Walter said he was going to play some basketball down at The Court to sharpen his skills. When he didn't return two hours later, I was worried. My husband phoned the police and they began a search. All they found was a Spiderman mask." She sighs audibly. Mr. Ware observes me intensely, wondering what I could possibly do to help that he has not already done.

Ignoring Mr. Ware, I scrabble 'Spiderman mask' in my black notebook. After Mrs. Johnson and I talk a little bit about the weather and whatnot, I ask, "That's all you know about the case?" I struggle to disguise my disappointment.

Mrs. Johnson glances at me with question in her eyes. Like she wonders if she can trust me. I want to tell her she can. "Well there was something else…" she states.

"Yes?" I lean forward eagerly.

"My husband received a phone call."

"Phone call?" For a moment I wonder if she just changed the subject.

"Yes," says Mrs. Johnson. "A phone call."

"From who?" I ready my pencil.

"Walter."

Investigations by Scout Williams: Book 1

"Your son?"

"Yes," she runs a slender hand with long, salon-painted fingernails over a thick blanket draped on the back of the light leather couch. "But he didn't say anything."

"He didn't?" I'm breathless. "Then who did?"

"No one," Mrs. Johnson's pine-needle eyes return to me. "No one was talking. It was just road noise. Road noise and heavy breathing. But it wasn't my son's breathing. It was someone else's."

"That's it?" My eyes feel like they will open no wider.

"That's it." Mrs. Johnson's eyes narrow. She catches her right elbow in her left hand. She crosses her feet at the ankle. "Now please don't tell anyone, Scout Williams." And then that convicting grown-up phrase: "I trust you."

My next statement comes out in a gush of exhaled and amazed breath. "Thank you so much."

"No, thank you for coming. It's nice to have someone to talk to at a time like this." She accompanies me to the door, her hand on my back, and waves as I ride my bike back home.

CHAPTER 5   *How the Rest of My Night Goes*

When I get home, a deliciously awesome smell wafts up my nostrils. Mmm. Spaghetti. *Mom's* spaghetti. I toss my notebook on the couch to the left and race into the kitchen. Mom's ladling out noodles and sauce in four bowls. "Can you please get Smith and your father?" she asks, examining the portion sizes with a hand on her hip.

I race off, sliding all over the polished wood floor. I find sixteen-year-old Smith in his room researching the Broncos' new quarterback on his iPhone. His room is small and messy with a little window. Pictures of admirable famous sports athletes like Peyton Manning and Michael Jordan line the wall, along with Denver Broncos posters and pictures of my brother as a little kid. In these photos, he has a baseball bat slung over his shoulder, and he's squinting as he smiles cheesily because the sun's too bright. Sometimes I wish I could have a room like this. All sporty and whatnot. "Time to eat," I tell Smith.

"Coming," he mumbles, absorbed in his phone.

Investigations by Scout Williams: Book 1

Next, I peek my head in Dad's office. He shoulders a phone to his ear, swivels around in his spinny chair, and holds up a finger. I nod, pretending to spoon food in my mouth, signaling him that it's dinner time.

Mom, Smith, and I wait a few minutes for Dad to show up. When he slides into his chair, we all fold our hands in prayer. As Dad prays, I wonder if God hears him. I stare at my spaghetti, wondering, *does He really care about my normal family and me?*

Dad finishes solemnly, "Amen." We all dig into our food. Smith slurps up a noodle and sauce goes flying. Mom taps his forearm and gives him the good manners look. He nods, wolfing down the food. I stab a piece of sausage with my fork and scrape it off with my teeth. I chew slowly, thinking about the eventful day. As if sensing my thoughts, Mom asks, "How was your day, Scout?" She rolls spaghetti around her fork.

"Good," I reply, shoving more food in my mouth.

"That's nice," she smiles.

"Tomorrow's Field Day," Smith announces triumphantly.

"No more school!" I exclaim.

"That's very exciting, kids," Dad looks up from his meal.

"What a hard-working family we have!" Mom exclaims, scraping the last of the spaghetti sauce from her white bowl.

Smith and I grin at each other and stand up with our empty dishes. Mom's always making comments like that. My brother rinses the bowls, and I put them in the dishwasher. Mom strategically situates the extra noodles in a container as she and Dad talk about

Investigations by Scout Williams: Book 1

work. I glance at the digital clock on the oven. It's seven. After the dishes are done and the counter wiped, I head to my room.

My room has a lot of windows and cream walls. Mom had hung up a bird picture when we first moved in two years ago, and it has never been replaced. Maybe because I'm too lazy to move it. Maybe because Mom likes it where it is. My bed, with its yellow blanket neatly situated on the lower half of the thin bedspread, is straight ahead when you first walk in, and the white dresser is on the left wall. I have a bookshelf/desk that is on the opposite wall loaded with books I have already read and several trinkets. I also have a Denver Broncos helmet that I confiscated from Smith's room when he was at summer camp on one shelf and a softball medal alongside. As much as I try and want my room to be athletic like Smith's, it simply isn't. Maybe it's because Mom won't let me. Several music trophies are dotted here and there. I didn't mention I play the violin.

I straighten up the bedspread and hang up some hangers that I had thrown around this morning. I pull out some PJ's from my dresser and I head to the bathroom in the middle of the hallway. Smith's room is directly across from mine. I slip on my pajamas in the bathroom that's in pretty good shape. At least *my* sink is in pretty good shape. Smith's has gobs of dried toothpaste on the sides and the silver faucet is spattered with white dots where spit missed the sink. I always dread to clean that sink when it's my turn to clean the bathroom.

After that, I discuss the mystery with Smith. He doesn't know any more about the strange kidnapping than I do. Finally, after watching a great horse movie called *Secretariat*, I flop down in bed. The details of the abduction swirl in my brain as I drift to sleep.

Investigations by Scout Williams: Book 1

CHAPTER 6   *After-School News*

The next morning is Friday, and I roll out of bed. *Only one more day of middle school left,* I encourage myself.

After a hasty breakfast of cheerios, I hop on my bike, backpack on shoulder, and pedal off to school. I don't let Smith drive me because I like the exercise and the fresh, clean air. Plus, Smith's crazy driving embarrasses me.

In about seven minutes of hard riding, I park in the school bike rack and scuttle inside the building.

My school is excellent. The outside's clean and crisp. The floors inside are shiny, and after you pass the two office doors on either side, the main hall runs right through the end of the long entrance hall where all the plaques and stuff are. At first, it's just straight rows of red lockers and giggling middle-schoolers. After that, a labyrinth of hallways lead to various classrooms.

Almost immediately, I'm sided by my friends Jennifer Daley and Constance Clark. Everyone we pass is buzzing about the

Investigations by Scout Williams: Book 1

kidnapping. Dexter Brown sidles up to Constance, Jennifer, and I as we discuss recent events. "Hey you guys! Did you hear?!" he asks.

"Yep," I say to the tall skinny boy as I toss my helmet in my locker and slam the door.

"Well I think Walt is gone forever!" He exclaims emphatically, planting his fists on his hips in a pose not unlike that of a superhero.

The bell rings loudly.

I nod to Dexter then race to class, tailed by Constance and Jennifer. *Does he* really *think Walt is gone forever?* That isn't the smartest idea I've heard.

My friends and I slip into math class as Ms. Mohren shuts the door. "Well," she glares at us over her glasses as we move into our seats. "We will do a review of algebra basics during our last period."

As she explains *x* this and *y* that my mind wanders to Walt. Where *is* he? Aspenvale isn't big enough to hide a kid for almost two days straight without anyone seeing him. But there *are* the woods...

Suddenly, everyone's staring at me. "Huh?" I sit up.

The class titters. Ms. Mohren glowers intensely at me. "I asked you, Scout Truth Williams, to tell me the golden rule of algebra."

"Um." I can feel my face turning red, and I tell it not to. *How does the teacher know my middle name anyway?* "Whatever you do to one side you gotta do to the other?"

Investigations by Scout Williams: Book 1

Ms. Mohren narrows her eyes then moves her wrath to another student.

Finally, the last math class of the year is over, and Ms. Mohren holds out a bucket of smarties. "Take just one," she says as we file out the door.

I'm tempted to answer, "Yeah we know, teacher," sarcastically, but I don't. This is my last day of middle school. Gotta make it count.

Next, I split from my friends and head to the science class to help Mr. Delano with one of his sixth-grade classes. I help him place candy at each desk along with a pencil that states, "You Rock," with strata layers all over it. Cheesy, in my opinion.

When the sixth graders burst in, everyone is loudly buzzing. When everyone is seated, there's only one empty desk. Walt's.

"He's been abducted by aliens!" A girl with glasses, pigtails, and a million freckles says in a mysterious voice, wiggling her fingers dramatically.

"Well, I heard he was shipped away to India to work in the salt mines," a know-it-all named Liv announces.

"There aren't even any salt mines in India!" a boy with swooshy hair rolls his blue eyes.

"Says who?" Liv folds her arms and juts her jaw at the boy, relishing the argument.

"I think he ran away so he could pose as a high schooler and try to get a job." Someone banters.

"Not as likely as he became a child model!" Liv yells.

Investigations by Scout Williams: Book 1

Mr. Delano interjects, waving his hands. "Okay, okay. Now I want each of you to say the most interesting thing you learned this year."

Silence.

Someone drops a pencil. Everybody stares. Mr. Delano gives me a look then declares, "Let's start with you, Scout."

I smile and talk about the brain and the nervous system. Kids start to nod, and Liv raises a hand. "You know, I really liked the science project that dealt with candy…" she says, nodding to assure herself.

Everyone looks quizzically at her. "What?" she shrugs.

I explain for Mr. Delano. "He means what you *learned* this year. You know, about actual science."

"Oh," she says.

The next half hour slogs by with kids saying cool science facts. I try not to fall asleep.

Now I'm sitting in an assembly, and the principal is speaking. "Students of AspenVale Middle, it's the LAST DAY OF SCHOOL! For you eighth graders, you're on your way to high school. I'm proud of you guys." Then, "You've got the whole summer ahead of you, kids. Make the best of it. See most of you next year." He then winks expressively to the eighth-grade side of the bleachers in the gym and dismisses us.

After a lunch of terrible hotdogs, Doritos, and ice cream cones, I sit on the benches and watch the sixth graders play a horribly disorganized whiffle ball game. Jennifer Daley plops onto the bench next to me. "What's wrong?" she asks.

Investigations by Scout Williams: Book 1

She startles me to reality. "Oh! Uh…Nothing. Just thinking about that kidnapped kid…"

"Oh, yeah…"

"Do you know anything about it?" I ask.

She changes the subject abruptly. "Are you excited to be done with school?"

"Oh…yeah." The bell screams its usual *bleep bleep bleep*. Only instead of sounding like a death wail, it sounds like angels singing because it's the final bell of the year. "I guess I'll see you later, Jennifer."

"Okay. Bye, Scout."

Riding my bike back home, I wonder what Jennifer is hiding from me. She had cut our kidnapping conversation short. I park in the garage and go inside. Mom has a very distressed look on her face. "Scout," she says.

"What's wrong?" I ask quickly, dreading what Mom will say next.

"It's the Jetson boys. They've been kidnapped."

Investigations by Scout Williams: Book 1

CHAPTER 7   *I Must Investigate*

I gasp. "All of them?"

Mom shakes her head. "Just Jefferson and Grant."

I melt into Dad's armchair and place my forehead in my left hand. "When?"

"Mrs. Jetson called about 30 minutes ago and said that when she called the boys in for family workouts, they didn't respond. Lincoln went down to The Court to get them, but they weren't there. All he saw was a white van with covered windows tearing down our street."

I shake my head, drag myself to my room, and collapse on my bed. *I have to find them,* I think. I flip to an empty page in my notebook and start compiling what I know and writing down possible suspects. I need to investigate more. I need to. It's not an option.

"Mom," I call as I dash down the hallway to the front door. "I'm heading out to investigate."

Investigations by Scout Williams: Book 1

She nods heavily as if her head weighs thirty pounds.

I slam the back door and crash down the hill, running the fastest across The Court, not wanting to imagine people peeking from behind trees or white vans creeping through the parking lot. I dash up the Jetson's hill and knock urgently on their glass back door. Lincoln answers, a worried look in his eyes. "It's just Scout," he calls over his shoulder.

Mrs. Jetson is distraught. She tries not to show it, but her voice shakes, and I can feel the turmoil in her heart. "Can I help you?" she inquires.

"I just want to ask some questions. Do you have a few minutes?" I ready a pencil and paper.

She nods wearily.

"When did you call Jefferson and Grant in for family workouts?"

"2:55."

She's very exact. I scribble it down, then turn to Lincoln. "When did you see the white van?"

"It drove off about three."

Mrs. Jetson shakes her head, her lip trembling, and holds back tears. "I thought they spent those five minutes packing their stuff. It didn't even occur to me that they were being kidnapped!"

Suddenly, a great idea zaps me. "Can I speak with Washington?" Mrs. Jetson casts a queer look but nods. Lincoln leads me up the spiral staircase and down a hall with what seems like a million doors. He knocks on one near the end.

Investigations by Scout Williams: Book 1

"Enter."

Lincoln opens the door slowly and reveals an eighteen-year-old sitting in a bean bag chair reading *Science for Nerds.* On his knee rests *The Key to Devastating Explosions.* He has thick square glasses, a buzz cut, and long, spindly limbs. This guy is Washington. "Scout wants to ask you some questions," Lincoln says, motioning to me.

He nods in my direction, keeping his eyes on the book as if it's so exciting he can't pull away from it. "Yes?"

"Did you happen to look out your window and notice anything unusual down at The Basketball Court?"

"As a matter of fact, I did. I saw these two men down there closing the trunk of an ivory van. One had on a mask. Then they leaped in and sped away." Washington likes to use hand motions. Then he adds, like he's in a school play and doesn't remember his lines, "I didn't know my brothers were in the van." He casts an uneasy sidelong glance at Lincoln.

"What did the men look like?" I write down everything he says.

"Uhm..." He seems uneasy. "Well, one had curly black hair and a beard...and, um, well I, uh...the other had on a mask."

"Thank you," I say, then follow Lincoln out as he shuts the door. "Has he been here the whole time?" We walk back downstairs.

Lincoln smooths his dark curly hair. "At 2:45ish, he went outside. Said he had to get a book at the library. I went with him."

CHAPTER 8   *Chick-fil-A Research*

When I get home, Smith sits at the bar counter, rubbing his face with his hands. "How was the last day of school?" He attempts a weak smile.

"Good." I don't even look at him. I am pondering the bizarre case. Why would someone kidnap Jefferson and Grant? Who would even kidnap *anyone*? "Smith..."

"Yeah?"

"Have you seen a white van with covered windows around?"

He squinches up his face in thought. All of a sudden, he snaps his long fingers. "On the way home from school, I saw one in the Chick-fil-A drive-through!"

Not sure how he remembers that. Why would he be gazing at Chick-fil-A while he's driving? That's self-explanatory, as Smith looks everywhere but the road while driving. Maybe the car Smith saw is not what I'm looking for. Maybe it was simply a Honda

Investigations by Scout Williams: Book 1

Odyssey and my brother's exaggerating. Maybe it was just an old Chrysler Town and Country van that gave my brother an unreliable chill down the spine. Maybe it was a Nissan NV that's really silver but gleams white in the sun. Or maybe it was the right van. The van I want. I'll have to trust my brother.

"When did you see it?"

"Probably 15 minutes ago."

"Can you drive me there!?" I ask. I know the mysterious customers are long gone by now but maybe the staff might have some description of the driver or passengers.

Smith nods quickly. We fly out the door and down the sidewalk to his battered silver Subaru Forester by the curb. Smith knocks it into gear, and we race off to Chick-fil-A.

He looks at me as he explains. "Ya know, dude, I would've given those guys in the van something to think about if I'd a known who they *really* were." He almost runs a red light and lurches the car to a stop. He continues to look at me as he drives straight.

"It's okay," I assure him, gesturing him to watch the road as he flips the turn signal on way too early. In about three minutes of constant *click clock click clock,* he jerks into the right lane by the edge of the highway. Did I mention Smith's a horrible driver? I mean, I don't even know how he passed his driver's test.

Finally, Chick-fil-A looms in the distance, and Smith stops right before the turn as if contemplating if he should turn or not. I hear the *squeeeeeeel* of someone braking behind us and several cars honk. Smith smirks and circles into the parking lot. I think he likes making people honk at him. Who knows why.

Investigations by Scout Williams: Book 1

Smith jolts to a stop so suddenly that I almost smash my forehead on the dashboard, my brown hair swinging around wildly. "You're a crazy driver," I state.

Smith smiles as if my remark is a compliment, although it isn't.

This Chick-fil-A looks new and kept up, with flower boxes outside the windows and fresh red paint. The drive-through menus are easy to read. Smith and I jog to the door and enter quickly.

It's semi-busy inside. A beefy young man smiles and waves us through the winding black tape that separates the ordering aisles. His nametag says, 'Stan.' "What can I get for you two today?" He asks, smiling all the while. *He must be a new employee,* I conclude. *He's very enthusiastic.*

"We'd like to talk to the drive-through people, please," I say.

"Attendants, dude," Smith corrects.

"Huh?" I'm confused.

"They're called drive-through *attendants*," Smith articulates.

"Whatever." I roll my eyes back to the waiting Chick-fil-A worker. "Can I speak to the drive-through *attendants*?" With this last word I cast a burning glare at Smith.

Stan raises his eyebrows—still smiling—at the odd request. "Sean! Stevie! Kids here want to see you!" He calls in a voice that sounds too young for his size and his age. I don't like it when high-schoolers refer to me as a 'kid.' I bet Smith feels the same way, especially since this guy isn't even a year older than him.

Investigations by Scout Williams: Book 1

Two Chick-fil-A *attendants* pop up next to Stan. Sean is a tall teenager with swishy hair, and Stevie, which is short for Stephanie, is a short energetic young woman with a silky black ponytail. Both wear red shirts and black pants. Stevie twiddles two Styrofoam cups in her hands, glancing at the drive-through window. "Yes?" They say at the same time. Stevie covers her mouth and giggles while Stan nods at Smith and me to commence.

"Have you guys served people in a white van with covered windows in the past twenty minutes?" I ask.

"Yeah," Sean replies, a little suspiciously. "They ordered like twenty-five sandwiches with like a million sauces."

A giggle from Stevie. I guess everything Sean says is gloriously funny to her.

"What did they look like?" I question.

"Well, there was this one guy with like a black beard, and another with like real short blonde hair and a mask. He looked, like, German. At least his hair did."

Stevie chortles.

"Did you see which direction they went in?" I continue. It's slightly annoying how Sean says 'like' so many times, and even more irritating how Stevie laughs at every single little thing he says.

"No," Sean looks at me like he is looking at some crazy psycho person. "I'm not a creep."

Stevie hoots and accidentally crushes a cup.

Investigations by Scout Williams: Book 1

I don't quite understand how seeing which direction a customer goes is worthy of the name 'creep.' I smile anyway. "Thank you!"

Sean and Stevie return to their jobs, and Stan—*still* smiling—lowers his thick eyebrows and nods.

CHAPTER 9 *Smith's Brilliant Suggestion*

When we arrive at home, Smith agrees to help me with the mystery. We pour over my compiled notes. Mom has gone to pray with Mrs. Jetson, encouraging her to trust the Lord and all that stuff. Stuff that's pushed to the corners of my heart. Stuff that's not altogether interesting to me. I *am* a Christian, but can't I be one without reading the Bible and praying to an invisible God? One thing I don't understand is God's justice. How can there be so much crime in the world if a just God is in charge?

Dad has to work till seven.

I don't feel hungry, but I still chomp slowly on a corn chip with hot red salsa, thinking. Thinking about Chick-fil-A, wondering how many of the restaurant's sandwiches Stan eats a day, pondering with capsizing guilt on my view of the Christian Bible and prayer. *I don't need it right now. I'll read a verse or two later. Maybe. Probably not. But God still loves me. Yeah, He still loves me.* The sound of *crunch, crunch, crunching* chips echoes across the house, as harsh and empty as my thoughts. Smith rubs his brow. "If only we could catch them in the act..."

Investigations by Scout Williams: Book 1

"That's it!" I exclaim.

"What's it?" He sits up, startled at my outburst.

"We catch them in the middle of kidnapping!"

Smith starts to get excited. "What if we camp out tonight?"

"Yeah."

"You can be playing basketball down at The Court to lure them in," he continues.

"Yeah?"

"And when they get close..."

"Yeah!"

"Bam! I'll catch them!" Smith claps his hands together as if he's smashing a fly.

"*We'll* catch them," I interrupt. I have to get *some* credit.

"Uh-huh!"

"Great idea, Smith," I grin.

Suddenly, Dad sweeps through the door. "Dad!" I'm so excited that I slur my sentences together, sort of hoping he won't hear the dangerous parts. "Smithhadagreatidea! Canwecampoutsidetonighttotrytosolvethemystery?????!!!! Pleasepleaseplease!?"

"Whoa, whoa, whoa," Dad titters, a little annoyed that we pounced on him and wrinkled his new navy suit. "Now, *what* are you requesting?"

Investigations by Scout Williams: Book 1

"We want to camp outside to get to the bottom of a mystery," Smith explains.

"What mystery?"

Smith glances at me, then answers, "The kidnapping."

Dad narrows his eyes and strokes his chin, a sure sign that he is thinking logically. "Now, I don't know if that's a good idea…" He stares off into space.

I gulp. Dad's answer is like waiting for the call that says you've won the lottery.

"And you're involved in this?" Dad squints at Smith.

My brother nods hopefully.

"I guess it will be a good after-school adventure…" Dad thinks that nothing will happen, that our plan won't work. "It'll be a valuable problem-solving lesson…" Fathers, always into the academic.

"So it's a yes?" I hold out my hands impatiently.

Dad's eyes twinkle, and a smile tugs the corners of his lips. "Yes."

I smile the widest smile in the history of wide smiles.

The sun is setting, so Smith suggests we head down to The Court. All we bring are a few blankets, a bag of chips, and my basketball, which was severely flattened until Smith pumped it up for me a few minutes ago.

I can tell he is as excited as I am, but Smith thinks that showing excitement is girly. And I'm not that girly, at least not the pink-sequin-twirl-dress-with-pounds-of-make-up kind who hang Taylor Swift posters on every square-inch of the wall.

We skitter into the small grove of thin aspen trees on the left side of The Court, my heart pounding. Can Smith and I catch the criminals without getting harmed ourselves?

CHAPTER 10   *The Villains*

It's dusk, and Smith forgot a flashlight. We decide that now is the time to put our grand illusion into effect. I casually slip onto The Court, dribbling the basketball leisurely. I shoot it at the basket, and it slams the backboard with a *ponk* sound, which makes me jump.

Smith kneels just inside the tree line, ready to pounce on anyone who attacks me. I keep glancing in all directions, which severely affects my shots. The eerie streetlamps by the parking lot make me shiver. I wonder who tells the kidnappers to nab children who are down playing basketball in a neighborhood park.

Suddenly, I hear the sound of a fast car racing down our street. Smith tenses and I start shaking. I tell myself not to be afraid, but that starts me thinking about what I'm even afraid of.

Brakes screech, and I imagine black tire marks on the new concrete parking lot. Do they belong to a creepy white van? I bounce the ball several times, and it rolls into the bushes a few feet from Smith because of my de-focusing skills. Which are high. He gestures for me to stay put. I nod faintly.

Investigations by Scout Williams: Book 1

Car doors slam, and I want to run and hide. Voices chat darkly, laughing. Suddenly, two men step onto The Court, and even their gait looks scary. They match everyone's description.

The first guy is shortish and stocky, with a stringy ponytailed beard. He has long hair and thick black eyebrows. He reminds me of a pirate, as he has a few teeth missing and disturbingly hairy arms.

The other guy has rigid hair; the moonlight glaring against it makes it look like rock crags. His eyes are blue and sparkle like diamonds. His face is covered with a new mask: one that looks like an old man. He has a harsh German accent. Everything about him is unsettling.

They both spot me and the one with the dark beard smiles wickedly. Both men quicken their walk. Black Beard rubs his hands together in evil anticipation. The Old Man laces his hands together and cracks his knuckles. *How on earth is Smith going to catch both of them? Call the police! Call the police!* I scream at him in my mind.

Smith is motioning wildly at me to do something, but what? I study his shadowy figure closer until he yells, "Ruuuuuuuun!"

But it's too late. I back into The Old Man. He snatches my forearms roughly, but I use a self-defense trick. I clasp my hands together and yank them up, breaking his grasp but sending me careening into the arms of Black Beard.

Smith joins the fight. He punches Black Beard under the jaw, and the villain reels backward. But the German guy is one step ahead. He grabs my arm with unexplainable force and tows me after him. Smith is still pummeling the other guy when he realizes that The Old Man is dragging me with surprising speed to his van.

Investigations by Scout Williams: Book 1

A puzzled, worried look enters my brother's eyes, and he races toward me. I try to plant my feet on the smooth concrete to stop myself from being taken somewhere I don't want to go. But Smith doesn't see Black Beard barreling toward him. *Oh God please help me and help my brother too and engulf these guys in a bolt of lightning.* Do I doubt God, or do I doubt my request? Is a bolt of lightning too much to ask from Him? But that's justice...and isn't God supposed to be just?

The heavy man lands on my brother in a running tackle. Smith's chin bangs the cement with a crack, and as the guy stands up, my brother lays limp. I start to cry angrily. This has all gone desperately wrong, and no lightning bolt from heaven has zinged down to make it right.

CHAPTER 11   *Carried Away*

The German guy shoves me in the back of his white van. I protest, yelling for help and wailing about Smith. Is he dead? The Old Man back-hands me across the mouth. Outside, a crow crouching on the telephone lines caws like he's a spectator of a comedy show or a ping-pong tournament. The distant moon just sits up there, bathing everything in its cold pale light.

The van is dirty. Scuff marks scrape through the dust, and white paint obscures the windows inside and out. The German stares at me, and the smile molded on the mask shoots a shiver down my spine. I look past him to the Jetson place looming on the top of the hill.

All of the windows are blank and dark except for one on the second floor. Is it just me, or is someone peeking through the drawn curtains?

I don't like the way The Old Man is looking at me, so I'm relieved when he shuts the trunk doors. And locks them. Never mind the relief part. The air is stifling. A tinted window separates

Investigations by Scout Williams: Book 1

the trunk from the two front rows of seats, and I can see both baddies hop in the van, kick it into gear, and careen up the incline to my street.

Stunned, I lurch backward, and my spine hits the doors harder than hard. I sit up, which is difficult because Black Beard is driving so crazy, and bang on the glass separator. *Fonk, fonk, fonk.* "Let me out of here, you creeps!! Letmeout, Letmeout, Letmeout!" I shout till my voice is hoarse.

Eventually, The Old Man turns around in the front seat and yells, "Halt! Shtop!"

I want to say something snarky in return, but instead, I just plop down on the van floor. Black Beard starts to drive normally now, I guess so he won't alert the police. I huddle up, gnawing my knees in white-hot fear. No lightning bolt. No angels. No loud voice saying, "Leave Scout Williams and her brother alone." Nothing. I am a grain of sand, as insignificant as a jungle gnat. I raise my head and peek through a place where the window is uncovered. Finding my brother. I'd rather have him here with me than unconscious on warm concrete. I see him, a lump of shadow in a world of shadow, disappearing through the small receding trees bordering The Court. Eventually I don't see him at all. The tears come. They make tiny oases in the dust that clogs the van floor.

It scares me to think how many girls have gotten taken like this. Snatched out of beautiful life and planted in a garden of terror. Girls forced to do things that are unspeakably evil. Girls sold like cattle in secret. Girls killed for the mere fleeting pleasure of killing. Which of the above will happen to me?

Investigations by Scout Williams: Book 1

We drive down Highway 89 and down a few alleys to a gravel road. The evil van jumps all over the place. *Where are we going, and what will these guys do to me?*

Soon, the van screeches to a stop, and the German guy jerks open the doors of my moving prison. "Where am I?" I demand.

He laughs harshly and peels off his mask. His teeth are white and straight, gleaming in the moonlight. He looks like an actor, and I wish he was one. His face seems chiseled, and his nose is perfectly shaped. My mind flits back to World War II, where the Germans thought they were the purest, the best, god-like. His eyes are breathtaking, clear as ice crystals and deep as Falcon Lake. The man relishes my amazement, and I wonder if he doesn't just wear the mask to hide his identity but also wears it to evoke this same reaction whenever he takes it off. "Karl!" Black Beard waves at him to come. Karl hesitates, then grabs my forearm and squeezes. It hurts so bad I almost yelp.

I dig my heels into the dirt pathway, making it hard for Karl to drag me up the rickety board stairs of some old cabin. "Schmutziges englisches Mädchen!" he mutters haltingly, spitting out each German word with every brutal yank of my poor arm. Black Beard pushes me through the cabin's open doorway and onto the dirty floor.

I lie there, thinking with dread how this is like some mystery novel come true. The last thing I see before passing out are Karl's white sneakered feet walking out of the door and hearing a slam that makes me cringe at the thought of the whole cabin collapsing on top of me.

Investigations by Scout Williams: Book 1

CHAPTER 12 *The Other Captives*

I wake up when I inhale some dust and cough violently. I stand up swiftly and examine my surroundings. The floors feel like I will plunge through them any second, and the termite-ridden wall's holes have been filled in with discolored spackling. The windows are painted over with black paint, so it's eerily dark. It's morning, and sunlight slices into the room through chips in the paint. There is a wooden chair in the corner, which looks like the unrepaired version of what Goldilocks broke. An old cot is thrown in the other corner, and a locked door with peeling paint leads to another room.

I yank on the doorknob to the other room, but surprisingly, it holds. I kick at the old wood, but more paint shavings just drift to the floor. I sit in a heap.

Whispers.

I freeze. "Hello?"

"Scout? Scout Williams?" The voice sounds weak.

Investigations by Scout Williams: Book 1

"Jefferson?! What? How? I mean..." I have so many questions, and all of them churned with the excitement of someone else in the other room—so close I can hear him—make me discombobulated. I wonder if Grant and Walt are with Jefferson.

Suddenly the front door flings open, flooding the room with bright morning sunshine. A man's shadow is framed on the floor. I slowly look over my shoulder. Karl. He's glaring at me with those eyes. "Oben!" he orders. "Up!"

I obey.

He slowly stalks over to me, scanning my face for forever, scowling. He shoves me so roughly that I tumble into the cot. A poof of dust makes me cough. Then he just walks out. "No talk."

I glare at him and wait until he's gone. Then I scurry next to the locked door and press my ear to it. "Jefferson, are Grant and Walt with you?"

"Yes...but Grant won't...won't respond to anything I do and Walt's all beat up. He vomited earlier and it smells terrible in here." Jefferson replies, obviously exhausted. He sounds pitiful, not the strong, dashing athlete he was just yesterday on The Court.

"What do these guys want?" I ask, watching the door warily just in case Karl barges in again.

"I'm...I'm not sure."

I slump against the door. What are Mom and Dad doing right now? Organizing a search party with the police? Is my brother alive? Tears well up in my brown eyes.

Investigations by Scout Williams: Book 1

CHAPTER 13   *Breaking In...and Out*

I wake up in a few hours, and it must be about noon. It's sweltering and stuffy in the room. Dots of sun are prying through the chipped paint on the windows. I try the front door. Still locked. So is the room the captive boys are in. I have to get out, but how? Suddenly an idea hits me like a crashing semi-truck.

I rip a leg off the decomposing chair and face Jefferson's door. I have to do this quickly, or Karl will hear. I take the deepest, longest breath I've ever taken and slam the door with my chair leg. The stick of wood snaps in half. So much for that idea. I pace the room, trying to conjure up another plan. How frazzled a person's mind gets when in danger!

Bingo! Racing to the old cot, I examine its metal legs. Wingnuts and screws attach them, I guess so it can be easily taken apart and carried. I twist the wingnut until I rub the skin off of my fingers, detaching a metal bar from the cot frame. I strike the door hard.

Investigations by Scout Williams: Book 1

It caves in a little. I hit it again and again and again, splintering a hole in the door. I take a nervous glance into the space. This room is smaller than the other and has no windows. The carpet is dingy, and the old-fashioned wallpaper is missing in spots. A terrible smell overwhelms my nostrils and I sway at the sudden onslaught of it. In one corner is a boy with hollow eyes and pale skin dotted with cruel bruises. Walt Johnson. In another corner sits Jefferson and Grant. Grant is sprawled on the carpet, unconscious, Jefferson kneeling over him with an anxious expression on his face. I widen the gap and slip through to the other room to help the boys.

Jefferson looks up at me like I'm Elvis Presley. "Hurry!" I shout. "We have to get out! This is our chance!"

Jefferson springs up, and I am so glad to see someone who is friendly that I almost hug him. But I don't because that would be weird. He appears uneasy too, like he is very glad I am here, but doesn't want to show it. He gestures to Grant.

Grant has the nastiest bruise on his forehead. I figure that's why he's unconscious. It's a mosh pit of sickening colors. Vomit green, grub yellow, wormy pink, and vampire-blood purple. I shake Grant's shoulders vigorously, shouting his name and explaining that we need to get out. Eventually, he comes to and touches his head woozily. "Stand up!" I jostle him to his feet. "We need to get out!"

Grant gazes at me, extremely puzzled. He nods wearily, not in agreement but because he can't keep his head up. Jefferson has already slithered through the hole and into the next room, and Walt is trying. I push him through, and after that, Grant weaves through the gap, followed by me.

Footsteps. They're the last thing we want to hear, but we all hear them.

Investigations by Scout Williams: Book 1

CHAPTER 14 *Breakthrough*

Jefferson braces the door, Grant and Walt helping. I retrieve my trusty metal bar and wait for the enemy to try to open the door. Soldiers, that's what we are. The good guys. The boys try to lock the door, but it keeps bouncing around from the forces pushing on the other side.

I hesitate. The opposing force is very powerful. Jefferson's sneakered feet draw thick lines in the dust.

The window!

On impulse, I smash the glass. Shards go everywhere. I jump through the window, the sharp juts of glass scraping me in a million places. The assailant realizes what is happening and darts from the door towards me. Walt sails through the window and lands with a painful sounding *thump* on the long-grassed ground. I help him up, and we both stare at the window, waiting for Jefferson and Grant. Jefferson appears and shouts, "Run! Get help!" He waves wildly for us to go.

Investigations by Scout Williams: Book 1

We hesitate, then Karl emerges from a grove of trees next to the window. We start sprinting toward the dirt road in the distance.

I chance a look back and see Karl, arms crossed, watching us go with his frozen blue eyes.

I run, run, run, tailed by Walt. I'm ever thankful that I had taken running classes from an Olympian. We stop at the dirt road, hands on knees, panting. I'm baking like a pizza, but the other kid is burnt to a crisp. We don't say anything, both of us too tired to formulate words.

Eventually, though, when I regain my strength, I ask, "It's Walt, right?"

"Uh-huh," he pants. His shirt is spattered with chunks of throw-up.

Down the road, we hear a loud truck coming, and it kicks up tons of dust. We wave our arms and shout from the roadside. I know better than to enter a stranger's car, but this is desperate.

The driver scrapes to a halt and leans to the passenger window. I can feel the AC from where I stand. "Ken Ah hep you keeds?" he asks with a Texas twang.

"Yes!" I answer. "We've been kidnapped and just escaped!"

"What? Geet in here and I'll take ya ta safety." Walt and I jump into the backseat of the baby blue Ford pickup and talk over each other. "Hode on, hode on, one at a tam," says the man, laughing like fifty-five-year-old men do to effusive kids.

Investigations by Scout Williams: Book 1

I explain the whole story, confirmed by nods from Walt, then add, "The crime scene is just up the road! We might catch them if we hurry!"

He spins the truck around, shooting gravel, dirt, and dust everywhere, and zooms to the dilapidated old house's driveway. Walt and I lurch in our seats. "Am Farmer Greenville," the driver introduces himself, his Texas accent sharp.

I smile in response as we pull to a stop.

The white van is parked in front of the house, and we race past it to the front door, which is slightly ajar. I burst into the room I had occupied not even 20 minutes ago and to the next. Not a soul. Farmer Greenville wants to search the whole house, but the door that leads out of Jefferson and Grant's room to the rest of the place is shut with a number lock. "I could bash a few more windows..." I suggest.

"Noh, we'll leave that to the po-lice." He says "police" in two syllables and pronounces the 'o.' I nod and race to search the van. Locked. *What's up with criminals and their locks?* I wonder. Both license plates are ripped off.

We all load back into Farmer Greenville's Ford and head back to AspenVale. Falcon Lake's large dam, framed by the Tetons, looms behind, casting shadow on the bouncy road. Pine, aspen, oak, and maple trees roam the land.

Walt takes a long drink of water. "Thanks for gettin' me outta there," he says to me as he wipes water from his mouth with his dirty sleeve. "My parents'll be real grateful."

I smile. "It was nothing." But with a remembering sigh I realize it was a lot more than nothing. A lot more. A twinge of guilt

Investigations by Scout Williams: Book 1

curls in my stomach when I realize that *I* jumped first out of the window. That I didn't stay to help Jefferson and Grant, the ones who *really* needed to escape.

We arrive at the police station soon after, me in a crypt of accusing memories. Mom sits in the waiting room. Her eyes get wide then spill over with tears as she rushes over to embrace me. A burly officer asks me questions, then drives Walt home. Mom expresses her thanks over and over again to Farmer Greenville, and he just slaps my back so hard without realizing it that I almost tumble over. As we drive down our street, Mom says Smith is fine but worried about me. We pull into the driveway.

It feels good to be home. It does not feel good to know I am a coward.

CHAPTER 15   *The Robbery*

I walk in the front door and grin. The fireplace to my left seems to smile at me, and even the dirty kitchen table looks welcoming. Smith sits in a comfortable chair, an ice pack to his forehead. "Scout!" he exclaims. "I'm soso sorry about this whole deal. That guy hit me so hard…"

"It's okay, it's okay," I reply. "It all worked out anyway." I race to my room and grab a pair of sweatpants and a Denver Broncos shirt. I then hurry down the hall to the bathroom Smith and I share and turn on the hot water.

This is going to be the best shower of my life.

My dripping wet hair feels good as it soaks the back of my shirt. I tell Mom the whole story, and she merely shakes her head

Investigations by Scout Williams: Book 1

and says, "I told your father when I got home from the Jetson's that it wasn't a good idea to let you guys roam around in search of dangerous men. We debated a bit, then I finally drove down to The Court, and all I found was Smith, unconscious, on the ground." She shudders, then gets that protective look in her blue eyes and holds up a finger. "Now, I don't want you down there anymore until the police find a solution." But then humble pride washes over the protectiveness in her eyes. "Oh but you were so brave helping those boys like that!" She closes her teeth together as she says it, like people do when they're so happy that they're crying.

"I don't feel brave, Mom. I jumped out the window first and didn't even stop to help Jefferson and Grant and Walt!" For some reason my eyes brim with tears.

"Oh hun you were perfect!" Mom takes my face in her hands. "I couldn't ask for a better daughter. You were so brave! Imagine the light of Christ you shined on those lost men!"

My heart wilts at this. I am certain that no "light of Christ" was displayed. No one that questions God displays his love or light. The shameful lightning prayer forms in my mind in fuzzy blue letters and I bow my head, cheeks burning. But then my corrupt soul fumes at the fact that God did not deal out justice to the terrorists then and there.

"You did just fine, Scout. Understand?" Mom affirms.

I nod, then ask for permission to go over to the Jetson's to reassure them that their sons are okay. She says fine, but as long as I ride my bike.

Investigations by Scout Williams: Book 1

I snap on my helmet and take off down the street. I have to ride a half loop to get to the Jetson's front yard since I can't just cut through The Court.

The wind feels good in my wet hair, and I even wish I'm not wearing a helmet so I can feel the refreshing air on the top of my head.

I park on the curb that separates the Jetson's yard from the street and hang my helmet on the handlebars. The place looks stunning from the front. On my left, there are three closed garage doors, and to the right is the cool front door, which sits on the other side of a wood-paneled curving wall. The roof is timber colored, and it's sloped in some parts and straight in others, almost as if the architect couldn't decide how exactly he wanted it.

I walk up the cement driveway, which is edged with perfect green grass, and bounce up the front porch's marble stairs. I rap loudly on the door, which kind of hurts because the wood's so solid. Footsteps.

Mrs. Jetson unlocks a million locks and peeks out at me. "Scout!" she sighs. "You're all right!"

"Yes, Mrs. Jetson, and I came to tell you that Jefferson and Grant are okay, as of a few hours ago."

Relief shoots across her face as she invites me in. "Tell me everything," she says. And I do.

At the part where I smashed the window, Lincoln moseys in and listens. Mrs. Jetson's face beams as I stumble through the part explaining how her boys let Walt and me escape. "Lincoln, were you up last night?" I ask. *Was it only last night that I was abducted? It seems like a millennia ago!*

Investigations by Scout Williams: Book 1

He seems disoriented at the question. "Yeah...I was watching a Marvel movie down in the basement."

"With who?"

"Dad and Washington, but I had a headache and only watched half." Both he and his mother seem amused at my questions, and that irritates me.

"Oh," I say. Just then, Lincoln's iPhone rings with a catchy song.

He answers it, and a weird look crosses his face. "Scout," he says, covering the speaker. "It's Smith. Says he wants to talk to you."

I accept the phone and say, "Hello?"

"Hey, Scouty, there's been a robbery at Chick-fil-A. I knew you'd want to find out what's going on while the clues are still fresh."

CHAPTER 16 *More Chick-fil-A Research*

I thank Mrs. Jetson and Lincoln for their time and dart out the door to my bike. I'm about to fasten my helmet on when Smith's familiar silver Subaru pulls alongside. "Chuck it in the back," he says, jerking his thumb backwards.

I follow his bidding then hop in the passenger seat. "You're well enough to drive?"

"Yep, but my head still hurts." Oh no. Extra bad driving today.

"How'd you find out about the robbery?"

"Saw it on the online news. It happened about 30 minutes ago." We drive lurchily down Main Street, past Gary's Gas and Flowers by Sheri, then park in the Chick-fil-A parking lot alongside three police cars with flashing lights.

We hurry inside and stand behind three people in line. In a few minutes, Stan waves us up and asks what we'll have. I feel bad for just asking questions again so I order a cookies-and-cream

Investigations by Scout Williams: Book 1

milkshake with whipped cream. As I pull three dollars out of my pocket to pay, Smith says that he will buy it to make up for last night. "Can I ask a few questions about the robbery?" I ask Stan. Five policemen debate in the corner, as well as Fox Ware, the FBI agent. He raises one sleek black eyebrow when he sees me, always glaring over the top of his sunglasses.

Stan raises his eyebrows and sighs out, "Sure."

"How did it happen?"

"Well…" Stan strokes his chin. "The window girl said that as she was checking out a customer, she noticed the register was empty."

"Had it just been emptied?"

"No, we do that after the workers switch shifts. She had just gotten off of lunch break."

"Can we talk to her?" Smith asks.

Stan sighs again and calls, "Vienna Daley?"

A college-aged girl with a frizzy French braid appears with a bag bearing the Chick-fil-A insignia. She seems exhausted but content. "Yes?" she replies curtly, unfolding the bag, ready to give someone a meal.

"Can we talk to you?" I ask.

"Of course." She glances at Stan, that annoyingly amused light in her eyes, and he nods.

We plop into a window booth and ask Vienna who she thought stole the money.

Investigations by Scout Williams: Book 1

She peels off her black visor and earpiece speaker and sighs. "I don't know what to think. No one I know who works here would ever do a thing like that."

"Who was on shift with you?" Smith asks.

She glances up and counts with her fingers. "Let's see here…There was Gerald and Shalie and Sam…and Curtis and Washington, not to mention Stan and Pete, who work at the counters. I'm a drive-through attendant."

Smith smirks at me because she said "attendant."

Slurping on my milkshake, I ignore him, asking, "Washington Jetson?"

"Say that again?" Vienna cups a hand around her ear. I guess it's hard for her to hear what I said through a mouthful of liquid ice cream.

I pronounce his name. "Wa-shing-ton Jet-son."

"Yes. One of the nicest people here. He bought us all sandwiches last Monday."

"Where was he on his lunch break?"

"With me. We sat here, actually, and we got through half the break when he said he was going to help a new guy at the window."

"Thank you, Vienna," Smith says. "We won't take up any more of your time."

She flashes him a brilliant smile, replaces her hairnet, and swishes back to her position flipping chicken nuggets or whatever a "drive-through attendant" does.

Investigations by Scout Williams: Book 1

CHAPTER 17   *Investigations by Scout Williams*

"Smith?" I ask.

"Yeah?"

"Could we drive out to Falcon Lake Dam and have a look around? It's so close to that cabin where I was imprisoned in."

"Sure, let's check it out." He swerves down an alley and speeds up a dirt road. We hustle down it for seven minutes, then pass the creepy old house that had been my prison just hours ago. I shudder at the memory of Karl.

Going further, Smith turns down a smoother road, Falcon Lake Dam towering over us. "This is the front way." Smith raises his voice above the engine and the *ping* of pebbles hitting the bottom of the car.

I nod.

"Now, where exactly do you want to look?"

"I'm not sure, maybe just off the road a little," I reply, then smile, staring off into space. "Investigations by Scout Williams," I accidentally say out loud in a dreamy voice.

"And Smith." He gives me that don't-forget-little-kid look; his eyebrows raised.

"We'll see," I laugh.

Smith pulls to the side of the road along a grassy ditch dotted with cute clumps of wildflowers, their heads bobbing like they're happy to see me. An empty police car is parked a little ways away. I guess the officers are out combing the forest for leads. I hop out of Smith's car. *What evidence could there be out here?* I wonder.

I trudge toward the woods, Smith following after he locks his precious car. Pine trees tower over us, and aspens wave greetings with their delicate roundish leaves. I'm admiring the late afternoon scenery, a glimpse of the white dam ahead through the majestic trees, when Smith exclaims, "Hey! What's this?"

I eagerly bound back towards him. "What!? What did you find!?"

He doesn't reply because he's reading something on a small strip of paper. I yank his arm down so I can see. It reads:

I'll bring the box tomorrow night, as well as the money. Are you sure what we're doing is right? Please reply via email.
Signed,

Investigations by Scout Williams: Book 1

CHAPTER 18   *More Clues*

"Box?!" I shout. "We *need* to find out about this box!"

Smith scrubs his chin. "Yeah...but I wonder who wrote this...definitely not your Karl guy..."

I snatch the scrap of paper and scrutinize it. "Nope. He can hardly speak English anyway. Who's 'J'?" A sunbeam streaks through a break in the forest foliage and bathes my hair in golden sunlight. "Jetson?! Is that who this is signed by?" I say, not believing it one single bit.

"Nah, those people are way too groovy," Smith replies, making a wave motion with his hands.

I stare at him, confused. "Groovy?" That's a new word in Smith's vocabulary.

"Yeah, you know like cool an—"

"We need to come back tomorrow night when the writer of this note comes with the box," I interrupt. "But first, let's check for me more clues."

Investigations by Scout Williams: Book 1

"Yeah."

I plunge into the long grass surrounding the clearing we stand in.

I scoot behind a blooming Juniper bush, and my hand slobbers across something wet. I pull back my hand swiftly and gasp. I don't like mysterious wet things. Smith grabs the thing and dangles it in front of my eyes. "An apple core?" I am suddenly interested.

"This isn't an apple tree," Smith observes, trying to sound detective-like.

"Well first of all," I look at him matter-of-factly. "This a *bush* not a *tree.*" I gesture to the Juniper bush we're crouching behind.

Smith rolls his amber, mountain-green hazel eyes. "Bush. Tree. Whatever. Basically the same thing," he says, scrounging for a phrase to make it sound like he knows what he is talking about.

I examine the apple core that Smith had dropped to the grass. It isn't even brown yet. "Somebody must've just been here!" I glance up at Smith with wide eyes, and he nods. The writer of the note.

It's funny how clues find their way to a detective.

Investigations by Scout Williams: Book 1

CHAPTER 19   *Unanswered Questions*

Smith and I drive home in the gathering darkness, both silent. Deep in thought. And I mean *deep* in thought.

"Are you sure you don't think 'J' stands for Jetson?" I ask my brother.

He looks at me curiously and shakes his head so vigorously he almost jerks us off the road. "No. So many *other* people with 'J' as a name live in Aspenvale."

"Meeowm," I grunt. 'Meeowm' means that I grudgingly agree. "When I get home, I'm going to search the whole phone book!" I huff. "But does 'J' stand for a first name or a last name?"

"Not a bad idea. Hey, what do ya think's in that 'box'?"

"Box?" My brain's so overloaded that all I can think about is the chili that Mom promised to make for dinner tonight.

"You know, that one in the note?" Smith realizes there's a stop sign ahead, and he erks to a complete stop, looking at me.

Investigations by Scout Williams: Book 1

"Right," I ponder hard. "Honestly, it could be anything."

Smith nods and resumes driving.

I growl despondently. "So many unanswered questions!"

"It's okay, Scouty," Smith simpers, adjusting the brightness of his headlights, which looks like a light show, while smirking at me through half-closed eyes.

"Don't call me that!"

"Okay, okay." We pull into the driveway, and I'm still thinking about the slip of paper I rub between my fingers. *Do people really write notes anymore? Can't they just call, text, or email? Why a note?* It looks like I'll have to deal with more unanswered questions.

We hop out, go inside, and devour huge bowlfuls of chili.

Investigations by Scout Williams: Book 1

CHAPTER 20 *Phone Calls*

After a nice shower and an industrious tooth-brushing, I beg to use Smith's phone. When he denies access, I snarl and ask Mom to use *her* phone. She agrees. I flip to the last name 'J' section of the AspenVale phonebook, which got thrown on our sidewalk a few weeks ago, and happen to look out at the moon hanging in the sky. What's keeping it there? God? Invisible cables? Gravity?

I sigh, still more unanswered questions. I reach last name *J* section of the phonebook.

The first person given is Jacklen, Carice. I dial her number, talk and listen politely, and hang up as soon as I can. She moved from California two months ago and kept complaining about how much better the oranges are there than they are here. I spare asking her about Walt, fearing she'll go on and on about the unfairness of America's leadership and how kidnapping could happen in the country.

Next, Newton Jackson answers the phone. He hardly knows anything about the mystery in the paper.

Investigations by Scout Williams: Book 1

After four more calls, I don't get any info. Frustrated, I punch Winona Jenridge's number into Mom's phone. "Hello?" Someone answers.

"Hi. I'm a local investigator." I control my frustration. "Do you know anything about the kidnapping in the newspaper?"

"Oh, dat? Well, I done read the whole doggone article and it says—"

"Oh, thank you, I'm just wondering if you know anything *other* than what's said in the newspaper. Were you out last night?"

"Well, missy, honestly, I don't think it concerns you. But if ya hafta know, I was at a movie last night with my friend!" Winona doesn't sound so happy that I'm all up in her business.

"Thanks, Ms. Winona, sorry to be a bother," I try to ease the tension.

"Oh, it's nothin', sugar. Have a good night!"

I hang up and sigh. *Still* nothing!

I notice Washington Jetson's contact, and I call it. Washington doesn't answer. I scribble his name from my list, even though a tug of questioning prods my gut. *Why, of all the names on this list, do I think Washington is a suspect? I just talked to him earlier. He told me what he knows. He knows what everybody else knows. White van. German man with a Spiderman mask. That's it. Why would he be any more involved than the other civilians I called? Why would he know more about this case now, just hours after I asked him about it?*

Next, I call Lincoln. "Scout!" he hisses once I explain why I'm calling. "Stop asking me weird questions!"

Investigations by Scout Williams: Book 1

"Okay, okay!" I'm shocked at his reaction. I tell him about the note Smith and I found in the forest near Falcon Lake.

"Well I don't snoop around in the woods and throw notes and apple cores around!" He says, exasperated.

"Well I'm sorry, Lincoln!" I apologize. "I just want justi—"

"Scout Williams! Leave me alone, alright? My brothers' kidnapping is a sensitive subject for me and my family!" And with that, Lincoln hangs up.

As I'm still reeling about Lincoln's outburst, Smith swaggers up from the hallway that branches to our rooms and points at me. "You need help with that?" he asks.

I jump at the opportunity. "Yes! Please! You can call these people on your phone." I scribble five names on a post-it note and stick it to the bill of his flat-billed hat. He's already taken a shower, but it's like that hat's glued to his head. He always wears it. Whether he has wet hair, dirty hair, dry hair, no hair. "I think Lincoln's the guilty person here. He just blew up at me over the phone." I muse.

Smith just widens his eyes, sighs, and sinks into the leather couch opposite me. He dials the first number I gave him. As it rings, he says, "Well what about Washington?' I sigh and call Jerry Johnson and tap my thigh as the phone beeps and beeps and beeps. A forty-year-old-sounding man answers. "Hello, this is Jerry, co-chef of Rigoli's Italian Cafe. How may I help you?"

"Hi, Mr. Johnson. I'm Scout Williams, your next-door neighbor. You don't happen to be related to Walt, the kidnapped kid, do you?"

Investigations by Scout Williams: Book 1

"He's my son."

"Great!" I realize that that word isn't the best to use considering the situation. "Were you involved in your son's kidnapping?" I continue.

"Say that again?" He says, confused. My implication is obviously out of the question.

"Were you involved in Walt's kidnapping."

"Miss, I think you've dialed the wrong number or something because I don't understand."

"Can I talk to you in person?" I know Walt's father doesn't sound guilty, but being the victim's dad and all, I think a meeting would be a good idea.

"Um, of course. Come to Rigoli's Italian Cafe at nine tomorrow morning, miss. And can I get your name again?" Mr. Johnson asks, clearly puzzled but polite.

"Yes, I'm Scout Williams," I answer, smiling so I sound happy even though I'm not. I'm frustrated. At everyone for not knowing anything.

"Nice talking to you, Scout. I look forward to our meeting tomorrow."

"Okay, thanks. Bye!" I hang up.

I switch to the first name 'J' section of the phonebook. After calling Jacqueline Grace and Jake Clinton, I still don't have any helpful information. There are only three people left to call.

Rocky Jru doesn't have anything.

Investigations by Scout Williams: Book 1

Florence Jotty doesn't have anything.

There's only one person that I have time to call; Mom needs her phone now. The name of this last person is Mason Judd. I can tell he's a teenager because of his gravelly voice. "What up," he answers.

"Hi?" I say, a bit self-conscious.

"Who's this?" he asks.

"Um, my name's Scout. I was wondering if you know anything about the kidnapping of Walt Johnson. You know, the incident that was in the paper a few days ago?"

"Huh? I don't read the weather forecast in the paper." Mason has better things to do.

"Weather forecast? I didn't say *weather forecast,* I said the *front-page article about the kidnapping of Walter Johnson.* You didn't listen to anything I just said, did you," I wave my hand back and forth, venting my frustration on the air.

"Nuh-uh."

I sigh. "Never mind," I answer, then hang up.

Mason hangs up without saying anything. I look up at the ceiling fans churning the air above as if the answers to my questions rest in them. Then I glance at Smith. He's in an animated conversation with some guy named Winston.

"Yeah!" my brother says, then waits for a reply, clutching the phone with both hands. "I know! The new War Zone game is like so cool!"

I hear an excited reply on the other end.

Investigations by Scout Williams: Book 1

"Right, man?" I hear my brother say excitedly. "I love the way you can upgrade to a new gun after playing for like ten hours a day! It's totally rad—"

I stop Smith in mid-sentence, slicing across my throat with my hand, a signal to stop. He speaks hastily into the phone. "Yep, see ya later, Winston!" He then hangs up and stares at me. "That was the last call."

"And?"

"This girl named Wylie Jewel knows where Karl lives."

"Really?!" *Finally!* Something worth my time!

"She said we could come over tomorrow."

"Cool." Tomorrow will be adventurous; I can feel it in my nerve endings.

CHAPTER 21 *My Nerve Endings Were Right*

After a fitful night's sleep, Smith and I prepare to leave for Rigoli's Café. Mom wishes us a good time, and we hop into Smith's Forester. I snap my seatbelt on and so does my brother. After typing Rigoli's Italian Café into Google Maps, he jerks off the brake and backs out into the street. When we start driving, I notice a blue Honda sedan behind us. *Huh. Never seen that car in our neighborhood.*

As our vehicle speeds into town, the mysterious car still tails us. "Smith." I don't know why I'm whispering. "I think we're being followed." Jerking to a halt, Smith stares into his side mirrors.

"It's Lincoln! Lincoln Jetson!" he exclaims.

"Let's stop and talk to him!" I suggest.

Smith pulls up by the curb and rolls down his window. "What's up, man?" he asks as Lincoln's passenger window slides down.

Investigations by Scout Williams: Book 1

"Nothin' much," our neighbor answers. I notice that he looks a little nervous, as his hands finger the steering wheel distractingly.

"Where'd you get that old car?" Smith asks. I roll my eyes. Smith doesn't know what he's talking about. This car is not old, it's brand-new. It still has car dealership displays in place of the license plates.

Lincoln laughs nervously. "Around." He pats the car's blue exterior.

I lean around Smith and ask, "Were you following us?"

"Following you? Pssshhht, no!" He narrows his eyes at me, tight anger in his voice. He revs his engine, the muffler loud. "Well, gotta fly!" Lincoln shoots down the street and blends in with the morning traffic.

"Weird," Smith sighs then changes gear, and we resume our drive to Rigoli's.

When we get there, we park in the gravel driveway. Rigoli's is a small restaurant with big windows.

Smith locks his Forester, and we walk to the glass entrance. The sign says the restaurant opens at eleven a.m., but a tall man is waiting inside. He unlocks the door and holds it wide open for us. "You must be Scout," he says. This is likely Mr. Johnson, Walt's father. "Ah, and who might this fine young man be?" he shakes my brother's hand warmly.

"I'm Smith." He pauses awkwardly, then adds quickly, "I'm her brother."

Investigations by Scout Williams: Book 1

"Nice to meet you, Smith. Now let's talk about your odd question, Miss Scout." He ushers us into a booth across from the door.

"Well," I explain about the note Smith and I found in the forest yesterday and that we called a lot of the *J's* in AspenVale. "I wanted to talk to you in person, since your Walt's dad and all."

"I see," the man strokes his stubbly chin. "Well, I was deeply worried when I heard about my son's kidnapping; you see, I left work early to search for him."

"So you weren't involved?" I ask.

"No, no, no! I love Walt with all my heart! I would never *dream* of hurting him or stressing out my wife!" he seems genuine.

"Well, I can check you off the list!" I laugh, crossing out his name in my notebook. *But can I really?*

"I'm glad you kids are searching for justice," the man stands. "Here, I just baked some breadsticks. Care to try one on your way out?" he nudges a basket toward us as we start for the door. We each take one.

"Thank you so much for your time, Mr. Johnson!" I call on the way to the car.

"No problem! Bring your family back anytime! We give special discounts to neighbors!" Walt's father waves.

"These breadsticks are good!" Smith says as we drive off.

"They sure are," I answer. "Are we stopping at Wylie Jewel's house?"

Investigations by Scout Williams: Book 1

"Oh yeah!" Smith swerves the steering wheel, and we barely make the turn into her neighborhood, which happens to be just to the left.

"How do you know where she lives?" I ask.

"Well." Smith's still chomping on bread. "She's my friend John's sister."

The Jewel place is a small, neglected yellow house with a splotchy yard. We park and knock on the peeling white door. "Hello?" a teenage girl answers.

"Wylie? It's me, Smith, and my sister Scout."

"Well," she pronounces the short *u* at the end of her *l's*. "If you're looking for Karl, he's over there." She points to a shabby house next door.

"Thanks," my brother tries to be nice.

She smirks like she's too good for us. By the time she shuts the door, I'm already on Karl's front porch. I knock as Smith dashes up.

A guy with long blonde hair, droopy eyes, and an always-open mouth opens the door. "Hey, dudes," he says.

"Um, hi," I stutter. "Are you Karl?"

"Bingo, man," he slurs.

"So you are Karl," I double-check.

"Yeah," he says, then looks past me to Smith.

I chuckle. "Sorry, but I think you're the wrong Karl."

Investigations by Scout Williams: Book 1

"Peace out," he says, then shuts the door.

"Well," I huff once we're back in the car, popping on my seatbelt. "Today isn't as exciting as I thought it would be."

"The day's not over yet," my brother says as we swing onto the highway.

"True." We pull into our driveway and head inside for a cold drink—Mom's running errands. I'm sipping my La Croix when I remember something. "Oh, I left my notebook in the car! I'll be right back!" I tell Smith as I jog out the door and down the sidewalk. I pull the passenger door open and retrieve my black journal. Rounding the front of the car, I notice a slip of paper squished between the windshield wipers and the glass. *Oh, just a piece of trash.*

But as I tear the paper from its spot, I realize it's *not* trash. On the bland, crinkled square of notebook paper, a note is written in neat black letters.

"**Williams kids:**" it reads. "**Stop Snooping! Or else you WILL regret it!**"

I inhale sharply. "Smith! Smith!" I holler like a wild man...or woman.

"What?! What is it?" He's worried.

I shove the note into his hand. I watch his face. As he reads the paper, his eyes grow round, and he gulps slowly. "Who would write this?"

"I don't know," I answer through clenched teeth. "But we're finding out tonight."

Investigations by Scout Williams: Book 1

CHAPTER 22   *When Darkness Falls…*

Later that night, Smith and I ready ourselves in the forest and wait for the suspicious character to show up with his mysterious box.

It's weird what happens when darkness falls. Animals jump about and have sing-offs, stars shine brilliantly above, and distrustful individuals do their dirty work.

Smith and I huddle behind the bush where we found clues yesterday. Waiting. Watching. Earlier, my brother had tried to get ahold of Mom and tell her where we were, but he didn't have cell-phone service. We figured she would know.

Suddenly, a flashlight beam lances through the evening blackness, and footsteps crash through the undergrowth. Smith and I zip our lips and swallow the keys. (Which isn't possible, by the way). Whoever the person is, he or she doesn't understand the idea of secrecy and crime. Turns out, there are *two* culprits.

Eventually, we hear a "Ssshhh!!!" and a sheepish "Sorry." Why are both voices familiar to me? The footsteps quiet down and

Investigations by Scout Williams: Book 1

two figures blunder into a nearby clearing, each tugging a corner of a large, cardboard box. "Sorry, Vienna, I really thought it was the other way."

"Well you thought wrong!" A female voice snaps back. Surely this isn't sweet Chick-fil-A Vienna, is it? "Just give them this thing, and I'll handle the navigating from now on."

Suddenly another voice enters the scene. "Have it?" Karl.

"Yes but I really think we should consider how this will affect—"

"Just give him the box, whine-bag," Vienna sneers. "You have a clue what this occupation will do to our lives? We'll be rich!"

"Box?" Karl pronounces the word deliberately as if it's hard to say.

"Yes," Washington says in a shaky voice. He and Vienna place the large box on the ground at Karl's feet.

"How much do we get?" Vienna snarls as if she has better things to do. She probably does. In fact, I *know* she does.

"JimBob said thirty dollars each. You will be paid more soon, especially after you finish that project for Chicago." Karl says, his accent making his words hard to understand.

"Thirty bucks!?" Now it's Vienna's turn to whine. "We earned more than that! Washington built this dumb thing with the money *I* stole!"

So Vienna stole the Chick-fil-A money!

"I cannot give you more. Meet me at headquarters in two hours so we can make our escape." *Escape!? From what?* With that, *Investigations by Scout Williams: Book 1*

Karl picks up the box, hoists it onto his shoulder, turns, and melts into the forest.

I fear he'll appear right behind us, and I jump when Smith whispers to me hoarsely. "We should follow him."

"Yeah!" I say a little louder than I should. I clap a hand to my mouth, my eyes wider than Mississippi Mud Pies. Whatever those are, anyway.

Vienna jerks upright. "You hear that?"

Washington nods, shaking uncontrollably.

"Let's go check it out." She grabs a large stick. Both of them head our way, Vienna whacking bushes, small trees, and anything that stands in her path.

"Run!" Smith whispers in my ear, pushing me to the side as Washington clicks on the flashlight and shines it in Smith's face.

I pick myself up and dart behind a tree to watch what'll happen to Smith.

CHAPTER 23   *Following Karl*

Vienna stares at Smith like she doesn't believe the sky is blue. "You!?"

"Yeah…" Smith sits up and rubs the back of his neck.

"What on earth are you doing here!?" Vienna spits the words like she wishes she could cudgel Smith senseless.

"You see," he starts. "My little sister was exploring out here, and she's, um, lost. Yeah. Lost."

"What did you hear?" Washington asks as if he fears my brother will eat him alive.

"Just things about money and boxes and stuff…Vienna, why are you so mean all of a sudden? I mean, you were really sweet the other day…"

I know Smith is stalling them so I can get away. I start picking my way through the woods after Karl. I don't hear the rest of the conversation.

Investigations by Scout Williams: Book 1

I can't see past a hand in front of my face, and unseen branches whip me unmercifully. I'm afraid that a spider will crawl into my hair or some sort of giant fly like the ones on nature shows will buzz into my mouth. I stop and listen.

Ahead I hear the faintest of faint woodland footsteps and I plummet toward them. It's probably Karl trying to retreat to his hidden fortress with his mysterious box. For curiosity's sake, I nose-dive toward the noise. Every minute or so I halt to listen to Karl's running footsteps. *Oh, how I wish I had a flashlight!*

A few feet ahead, I detect a creepy white light. I hurry over to find myself blocked by a close wire fence, electric barbed wire lining the top. It's at least 8 feet tall. I gape and peek from behind an alder tree. No way I'm climbin' that unless an elephant knocks it down for me.

Karl rushes out to the gravel surrounding the fence and pulls out a ring of keys from one of the million pockets on his khaki cargo shorts. He keeps glancing over his shoulders anxiously. His breathtaking eyes contain a worried look I've never seen on him before. Karl unlocks a gate about twenty feet away from me and dashes inside, quickly locking it behind him. *How am I ever gonna get inside that?* I ask myself.

I study the imposing gate, wondering how to get in. I wish I had my trusty metal bar that I smashed the old house's window with so I can bash the fence to shreds. Then I get an idea.

A tall aspen towers above the fence, and I figure I can climb it and bend it down over the fence so I can jump to the gravel on the other side. But that only happens in movies. I try to conjure up another plan.

Investigations by Scout Williams: Book 1

CHAPTER 24 *The Real Plan*

Just as I'm mulling my options, JimBob stalks out of a door in the large white building inside the fence. He calls to Karl, who is digging in the backseat of a truck. "Karl!"

The blonde man whirls around and tosses the big box to JimBob. JimBob catches it, almost tipping over at its weight and sniggers. "We'll blow the place with this baby! Hehe!"

"Yeah, man!" Karl has dropped his accent! "When we gonna get outta here?"

"Tonight after we plant them bombs and dynamite in that dam."

I don't understand; JimBob and Karl are trying to blow up Falcon Lake Dam!? Does Washington's mysterious package contain a bomb?

"What're we gonna do with those kids?" Karl slams the truck door.

Investigations by Scout Williams: Book 1

"Leavin' 'em here. Can't afford to buy 'em any more Chick-fil-A sandwiches," JimBob jokes evilly.

Karl laughs. "Now I can drop this dumb German accent!"

JimBob peeks in the package from Washington, and a disgusted look crosses his face. "Where's the T&T?"

"Isn't it in there?"

"No!"

"I can run to the store…" Karl offers.

"Noh, I can do it. Ya don't know where the specialty shop is. Watch them kids and make sure no one breaks 'em out." JimBob hops into the pickup and pulls up to the gate as Karl unlatches it open. The truck zooms past me and down a dirt road in the direction of AspenVale.

All of a sudden I hear a *diiiiing*. Karl leans against the gate and pulls out a cell phone and starts texting. This is my chance.

I slip from my hiding place and tiptoe through the gate. I turn around to make sure Karl hasn't seen me.

He stares at me with his iceberg eyes.

CHAPTER 25   *The Chase*

Karl shoves the phone in one of his pockets and dashes after me. My heart jolts, jumping into my throat. *Dumb idea! Dumb idea! Dumb idea!*

I sprint through the gravel to the bleached building. Karl grabs my shoulder, but I tear away and fling the nearest door open. His fingers leave stinging scrapes on my shoulder and down my shoulder blades. It's dark inside, but I don't care. I slam the door behind me and run as I have never run before down the smooth hallway. I jolt another door open and skid in. It's an office of some sort. I'm looking around when a door on the other side of the room whooshes open and Karl lunges in, his eyes wild. I try to scream, but nothing comes out. Fear grips me in its clawed grasp as all of the horrible things Karl will do run through my mind.

I tumult through the way I had come, Karl close on my heels. I fly down another hall, my Nike sneakers squeaking on the shiny floor. I look behind me, but Karl isn't there. My heart almost does a belly flop to the floor as I realize he's probably going in front of me so I'll run right smack into him.

Investigations by Scout Williams: Book 1

I try a door. Locked. Another door, and it leads me into a small dark room littered with boxes and crates and bins. The perfect hiding place. I burrow through a pile of boxes until I find an empty one that I can fit into. I melt underneath it, trembling so much that I think the box is quaking like an aspen leaf.

I peek through a small hole at my eye level. Even though I expect the door to open, I almost jump out of my poor skin when Karl crashes in, scattering boxes everywhere.

I shut my eyes and pray. This is the first time I have even considered asking for God's assistance. Can He really help? No, *will* He really help? Will He be just? A strange idea flickers in my mind, and I know He will help. He will have His justice. A Bible verse flashes into my head. *Isaiah 30:18. 'Therefore the LORD longs to be gracious to you, and therefore He waits on high to have compassion on you. For the LORD is a God of justice; how blessed are those who long for Him.'* God doesn't zap people because He wants them to have a chance to come to Him. He is both loving and just. I start to pray desperately, my emotions, hopes, and apologies mixing and mashing into one great appeal to my Creator.

Karl glances around, his eyes no longer like ice but like blue fire, and I think he's staring straight through me. But thankfully he's only having a stare-down with the box and he huffs out and shuts the door so hard I hope it won't break the walls down. God *did* help!

I get a sensation that I'm being protected. I've never felt this way before, but I know it's God. *Please protect me from this evil man. And watch over the Jetson boys too,* I pray. It feels great to have someone to confide in.

I wait for Karl to leave, then quietly take off my box. I maneuver around upturned bins and crates and peek out of the

Investigations by Scout Williams: Book 1

small foggy window into the hall to make sure he's *really* gone, then slowly I unlatch the door. When it clicks I hold my breath. I tip-toe down the hall, checking and listening at every door, trying to find Jefferson and Grant.

I cautiously slip down some iron stairs and into *another* hallway. *How many hallways does this place have?* I jiggle a door handle.

"Mm! Mm! Mm!"

What in the world?

"Mm! Mm! Mm!"

I pick up a piece of wire lying nearby and shove it into the lock. Nothing but more 'Mm's. All of a sudden I hear a door slam and I look back. Karl has come inside and he shuts the door to the top of the stairs behind him. He plods slowly down the stairs, a Glock 9mm handgun clutched in his hand. I press my back to the door and slide to the floor. *What will he do to me?*

CHAPTER 26   *The Grate Our Last Hope*

Karl stalks over to me. I shake violently but try to be courageous. I stand up slowly, looking him straight in the eye. "No move." He restores his accent.

"You don't need to use the accent anymore. I know you're not German." I will my voice not to shake.

Karl looks so mad I think I see smoke curling out of his ears. He brandishes his huge ring of keys and unlocks the door next to me. "I don't like snoopers," he sneers, then rams me into the dark room.

I hit the floor hard and it hurts. Really hurts. *Snoopers. Just like the note on Smith's windshield.* The dust makes me cough and the *clang* of the slammed door rings in my ears. I sit up, my hair hanging in front of my face, and peer around. I jump at two pairs of eyes staring at me. Jefferson and Grant!!!

I smile and drag myself over toward them. When my eyes adjust to the darkness, I notice both boys are chained to a ring on the wall and have black cloths cover their mouths. Grant's forehead and right eye are more swollen than ever and Jefferson looks like

Investigations by Scout Williams: Book 1

he's about to pass out. Karl has made a mistake locking me in here with them; now I can free them, or at least try to.

I hurry over to Grant and untie the cloth from his mouth. He gasps and breathes like he has asthma. I take off Jefferson's cloth as well. The look in his eyes says, "Thank you you're the best person in the world right now." I smile thinly and sit back against the wall alongside him.

After a few minutes of silence in the dark dusty room, Jefferson starts to speak. "Scout, we have to do something. They're going to blow up the dam."

"And ya know what that means," Grant adds, fear riding his voice.

"There're really going to slaughter the whole town? What about us?" I exclaim, the awful realization hitting me like a train.

Jefferson nods grimly. "They're leaving us here to die."

"That water will destroy the whole town!" I choke. "*Everyone* will die!"

Both boys remain silent. We have to think of something fast. I jump up and bang on the door. "Let us out! Do you realize what you're doing?" But Karl is long gone.

I sink to the floor. The boys look at me mournfully. "Thanks for trying." Jefferson offers a weak smile. But I'm not looking at him. There's a grate in the right corner.

"What's that grate for?" I ask, suddenly curious.

Grant shakes his head. "Probably a heating vent," Jefferson says. "What's your idea?"

Investigations by Scout Williams: Book 1

I head to the grate and pull it out. Luckily it isn't bolted and it's pretty big. "Wait here. I'll get Karl's keys and get us out of here." Grant opens his mouth and Jefferson looks at me with adoration. I gulp, pray there will be no spiders, and crawl inside. "Pray!" I whisper back at them. They nod and shut their eyes.

The space inside the grate is tight and I barely fit. On any other occasion this wouldn't be necessary, but it is now. It can't always be daisies and lollipops.

The metal walls of the vent are confining, and I wade through dust piles. I wonder if I will ever get out. *If I do, will Karl be waiting?* He seems to sense that kind of stuff. I can't blame him though, with his deep blue eyes and orthodontist commercial smile...I inhale some dust and possibly a dead gnat, which brings me back to reality.

I clamber down the eerie space and turn left, trying to follow my mind map of the building. I'm soon confronted by a metal wall. Great. Looking up, I see a pinpoint of light. I take a deep breath and put my feet on one wall of the vertical vent and my back on the other. I then shimmy up the claustrophobic tunnel, telling myself not to look down. When I reach the middle of the vertical shaft, I scramble down a horizontal vent that snakes to the left, deciding not to continue going up. Ahead is another grate. Thank the Lord for heating vents. I kick it open and recognize the hallway as the one by the office. Perfect.

Investigations by Scout Williams: Book 1

CHAPTER 27 *Conversing with Karl*

I peek into the office via the small window on the door. Karl is inside messing with some sort of timer looking thing. My heart skips a few beats. I open the door and walk in like I'm entering Smith's room. Karl looks up quickly and nearly drops the object he's messing with. "How? What?..."

"Karl," I plead, my voice shaky. "You don't have to do this." His eyes looking straight into mine nearly make me faint. "Please let my friends go."

He walks over to me. I hope he won't grab me or something. Silence. "How?..." he begins.

"The heating vent." I shrug like it's no big deal. "Karl, why?"

His eyes harden and he snarls, "Listen, girl, if you don't get out right now I promise I'll hurt you."

"I'm not scared." But I am.

"I'll give you one more chance to run," he shakes a finger at me, Mom style. I take him up on his offer. On my way out I snatch

Investigations by Scout Williams: Book 1

Karl's key ring, which rests next to a new mask, from off one of the white tables and dash out. I slow down a little once I'm a safe distance away from the room and look behind me, only to find Karl zipping toward me. I know he hadn't been joking when he said he'd hurt me. I find the open vent and hurry inside, my heart pounding.

Karl grabs my foot and I can feel myself sliding. My fingernails scrape the metal as I try to hold on. Karl turns me over on my back and yanks my other leg. My head slips off the opening of the vent and hits the floor with a *crack*. I feel dizzy and my vision blurs for a second. Karl grabs the collar of my shirt and lifts me to my feet. I feel like gagging. I struggle wildly. Karl's face is contorted into an anticipating, scary scowl. I yelp out a short, choked scream. Then, as my feet find the floor, I rear back and kick Karl in the shins. He grunts and his face melts into a ridiculous look of surprise. Taking the opportunity, I uppercut him directly in the chest, as I'm too close to effectively get to his face. He twists back his arm for a return strike. I duck, and in so doing sprawl on the floor. Karl sees me caught off guard and grabs my arm, lifting me up.

My heart swings wildly against my ribs, and my breath comes out in short, scrambling spurts. It's not the painful squeezing Karl applies to my upper arm that makes me short of heartbeats. The truth is, I'm afraid I'll never see my family again. I'm afraid I'll never see Jefferson and Grant for the last time. Karl's voice breaks my thoughts. "Now I have you." *Is his voice the last thing I'll ever hear? God*, I pray, the words swimming in my ears like schools of fish. *Why is this happening? Please...help me. Please.* Then I add something that, strangely, comes from the depths of my heart. *If it's Your will. Only if...it's Your will.*

I wonder what will happen to me. Endless possibilities swarm in my head. Caught off guard, again, by Karl, I'm rammed

Investigations by Scout Williams: Book 1

into the wall. My head bangs loudly against it and throbs painfully. Karl begins to walk, pulling me behind him. He drags me into an empty room with nothing in it but a few wooden crates and a rusty crowbar.

I take a sad glance back at the empty, uncovered heating vent, which I can still barely see through the open door. I wonder what will happen to the Jetson boys.

CHAPTER 28   *Fight for Life*

All of a sudden, Jefferson pokes his head out of the dusty vent, his face a mix of terror and worry and fear. He notices me in the room and his mouth widens.

I don't know what to think. *Should I warn him that Karl is ready and willing to fight? Should I be happy he's here?*

Jefferson and I hold a second-long, silent conversation.

What should I do? his eyes ask.

Something, I answer with mine. *Do something. And quick.*

I vaguely hear Grant behind his brother. "Go, Jefferson! I'm waiting!"

Karl's head swings around at the sound of Grant's voice. He snarls when he sees the Jetson boys unfolding out of the vent. He shoves me against the wall with one powerful fist clenching the shoulder of my shirt. He eyes the Jetson boys.

Investigations by Scout Williams: Book 1

I look straight at my friends. They both stand there, and then Jefferson starts running toward us. A sudden wave of adrenaline pumps through my heart, and I viciously attempt to shoulder Karl's hand off me. Karl snarls as I struggle. When I finally get out of his malicious grasp, he grabs for me again and catches my wrist. He drags me into a room scattered with crates. But as the Jetson boys get closer, Karl realizes he can't hold me back and fight off the boys at the same time.

Leaving me bruised and gasping, Karl turns around to face Jefferson and Grant. He grabs Grant's shirt and throws him hard to the floor. Karl swings at Jefferson, who ducks sharply.

I have to help them! I scan the room desperately. A crowbar lies amid the crates. I grab it up. I rush toward Karl.

He turns around as I swing the large weapon. He ducks. The crowbar flies over his head and takes me with it. Off balance, I thrust my makeshift weapon into Karl as he towers over me. Jefferson hauls himself off the floor and wrenches him backward so I can get up. I rear the black crowbar back and wham it hard on the side of Karl's head. He flops down on top of Jefferson and me, out cold. As I disentangle myself from Karl's limp arm, I ask nervously, "Is he dead?"

"No," says Jefferson. "We have to get away before he wakes up."

All of a sudden, a crash echoes through the building. Karl's eyelids flutter.

"Hurry!" I whisper hoarsely. Then, I skid out of the room and enter into the next door to my left. The boys follow. I shut the

Investigations by Scout Williams: Book 1

door quietly once we're all in. I shut my eyes in relief. *I hope I never see Karl again!*

Grant's breath comes out in short rasps. The sound seems loud to me. "Sh!" I warn. He quiets a little, closing his mouth.

Suddenly, I hear a shout echo off the stark walls. The boys notice it too, as they crane their necks to hear better. "Karl!? Karl!" JimBob.

"Yeah?" Karl shouts from nearby, startling us. The boys and I link eyes. We hear the man shuffle to his feet, muttering.

I take a quick peek out the small window on the door. Karl staggers toward the voice of JimBob.

"Let's go!" JimBob yells. A few seconds later, I hear him say "There you are!" as he sights Karl. A door slams in the distance. A motor starts.

Jefferson, Grant and I get up. We dart out of the room and run and run and run, heading to the way out of this nasty place. "Come on, guys!" I race to the entrance, which is in sight. A white truck is kicking up dust as it barrels down the road toward the dam. There's only one option, the van that had been my transportation to every horror that every teenage girl has.

"I'll drive," Jefferson smirks.

Investigations by Scout Williams: Book 1

CHAPTER 29   *Following JimBob*

Jefferson bangs on the headlights and slams the stick shift into gear. Grant and I hop in the passenger seat. I hand Jefferson Karl's key ring and he inserts the fourth one he tries. He backs up jerkily and Grant bangs his swollen forehead on the dashboard. "Aow," he moans. I can tell it hurts, though he tries not to show it.

"How'd you guys break out of those chains?" I shout over the crunching sound the van makes as it speeds over the gravel.

"Just...pulled our hands out of them," Jefferson shrugs. "It took some effort." The moon highlighting a wry look on his face, he holds up a fist to show me the dark bruises covering his wrist and forearm. Grant's wrists are the same.

Looking closer, I find both boys are spread with bruises, and crimson blood trickles from Jefferson's nose. One of his eyes is swollen shut, and I look away. All of that pain for me. Sacrificial love. Like Jesus' death on the cross for our salvation.

Jefferson is soon going 70 miles an hour down the dark road. Dust still hangs in the air from the criminals' truck careening down the road ahead of us. We stop in a grassy clearing that had

Investigations by Scout Williams: Book 1

been made into a parking lot alongside the white Chevrolet pickup. The sound of water reaches my ears. We rush out and down a primitive trail, which is hardly visible in the midnight starlight. The trees open up before us and I catch my breath at the sight of the dam. It's an invincible white wall at least 100 feet high. A waterfall shoots out of the dam, creating a river that cuts through the forest. White vapor blankets the dark, starry night like a hazy stratus cloud. I notice stairs near the side and sprint toward them.

Tall white streetlamp-like poles illuminate our path. We take the white stone stairs two at a time, me tripping at least a hundred times, and end up on a balcony overlooking the forest below on the left and the vast expanse of Falcon Lake on the right. My heart quickens at the thought of what will happen when all that water plummets down and ends hundreds of lives.

JimBob stands in the middle of the walkway. Grant hangs over the railing, searching for the bomb. He doesn't find it. White, cold steam-like vapor rises hauntingly. *Where is Karl?* I think to myself with suspicion.

My thought is too late. I am snatched from behind. "Scout!" shouts Jefferson.

"Oh no, young man, don't even try to save her. Don't even try. There is no rescuing this girl. No." He clenches my arms with his hard hands.

I scream. The boys' faces twist in anger.

"Karl! Timer's on!" JimBob warns.

Karl doesn't reply. He drags me to the edge of the dam. The Falcon Lake side. Both of us stare into its blue depths. Me with dread. Him with triumph. "You're going in kid," he rasps.

Investigations by Scout Williams: Book 1

This guy has gone completely crazy!

"Say your goodbyes, Scout Williams."

My eyes meet Jefferson's. He knows if he tries to help, I die even quicker than intended.

"Scout..." Grant says softly.

Karl lifts me over the metal railing. Nothing separates me from ten feet of open air before hypothermic water. Then he lets go.

Investigations by Scout Williams: Book 1

CHAPTER 30 *Five Minutes*

I watch the dark surface of Falcon Lake rush closer and closer, my dread mounting and my heart slamming rapidly. I close my eyes and suck in a deep breath.

I plunge into the icy depths of the lake, and my heart seems to give one more resounding pound before stopping completely. I swim up. Up and up. I wonder what kind of terrifying, nocturnal creatures live in these waters. Do any of them eat humans?

Finally, my head breaks the surface. I take in long breaths, treading the dark water to stay afloat. "Scoooouuut!" comes a long cry from above. I cock my neck far back to see the top of the dam. Both Jefferson and Grant lean over the rail.

"I'm here!" I call wearily. "I'm fine!"

"Good," Jefferson replies. "Scout, the bomb's underwater."

"What?"

The boy points down and to his left. "See that blinking red light? That's the bomb!"

Investigations by Scout Williams: Book 1

My bangs sit straight on my forehead, nagging my eyes. I strain to see the light. There it is, a faint blinking red carried by the smooth ripples of Falcon Lake.

"How long do I have?" I peer at the brothers' silhouettes. I must do something.

"Five minutes," calls Jefferson. "Only five minutes."

"Good news, Scout!" shouts Grant, waving around something in his hand. "I got Karl's phone! The police are on their way!"

"Great!" I try to sound happy.

"Scout," Jefferson cups around his mouth to be heard. "Would you like me to jump?"

"No! Find high ground! I'll be fine! I promise!" I smile reassuringly, then realize they can't even see it.

I take off swimming. Ploughing through the water in a flailing sidestroke, I soon realize how tired and beat-up I am. I feel drained, like my energy is the swirling water in a bathtub with an unplugged drain. The light gets closer, brighter. I know I'll have to go underwater to see the bomb. I get to the wet, white side of the dam. The bomb is directly below me, stuck to the wall. Taking a deep breath, I sink down into the water a little, then open my eyes.

I can hardly see anything, just the way the moon plays in the water and the repeated flashes of the red light. I find the bomb, an ugly contraption. Numbers blink. 2:48. 2:47. 2:46. I bob up for air, then surface dive back down.

The sound underwater is eerie. An aquatic noise, broken with occasional flicks of electrical-sounding ticks. Panic ensues. 2:15.

Investigations by Scout Williams: Book 1

2:14. I touch the bomb. It feels cold, hard. It is about as long as one of my outstretched arms, and thick as a typical sized Amazon box. It is sleek, with wires and plastic and twisted cords sticking out of it at certain places. I wonder how to shut it down. Is there a way? Am I about to die? *Lord, please help me!*

1:30. I, frantically, rise for air then return. I feel around the bomb. I pull cords and wire. Nothing happens. I try to pry it from the wall, but I can't. It is stuck there. 00:59. 00:58. 00:57. I search every inch of the thing but I see nowhere that implies power-off or shut-down. 00:41. 00:40. I trace the outside of the bomb and notice a fine wire that shoots down. I follow it with a finger, then see a little circle that glows a faint red. It's a rubber button. It's unlabeled and very mysterious looking. I dart to the surface for air.

CHAPTER 31   *Five Seconds*

From the surface, the little button is a lot deeper than I anticipated. I pass the bomb. I have eleven seconds. I swim down as fast as I can, my lungs feeling as much pressure as my body. I lose the thin wire once in panic but find it again.

I have only nine more seconds.

I find the button.

I have only seven more seconds.

Am I sure this is a cancel button? What if it makes the bomb explode immediately?

My ears feel stopped up, and one of them clears with pressure. I press the button. I wait, listening.

Nothing happens. Nothing. I open my eyes. The bomb blinks 00:05.

00:05. I shoot to the surface. I smile genuinely. Then I wonder how I'll ever get up.

Investigations by Scout Williams: Book 1

The police have arrived. Their sirens blare. Faint talking, faint radio noise. I tread water wearily, wishing I had something or someone to hold onto. I shut my eyes.

Noises directly above startle me. "She's down there!" Grant.

"She was thrown in." Jefferson.

Waterfall noise flows, a soothing sound.

"Hello down there," calls a police officer.

"I'm here," I answer weakly.

"Young lady," says the officer. "We're sending a boat out to retrieve you. Hold on."

I nod, though I know they can't see it. Soon, I hear a boat come motoring toward me. Its shape grows larger, and sparkles in the moonlight. Two figures wait inside. Jefferson and an officer.

I smile as they approach. "Thank you," I breathe, exhausted.

They both lift me into the boat. I am sopping wet, my clothes shiny and dripping from the water saturating them. "Are you okay?" asks the stout, middle-aged officer who maneuvers the boat. "Any injuries?"

"No sir." I shake my head.

Investigations by Scout Williams: Book 1

"You did it, Scout." Jefferson whispers, hugging me. "You did it."

I feel like falling asleep. My hair feels ratty and sticky. My eyelids feel heavy.

I fall asleep.

CHAPTER 32   *Daniel Stockire and Tommy Jacobsen*

When we land on the shore in a small clearing, I wake with a start. The other policemen and Grant rush to us. As I explain to the police that we have to stop JimBob and Karl, Fox Ware materializes out of nowhere and sets a surprisingly heavy hand on my shoulder. "Nice work out there, Scout Williams. I must say, you did surprise me. I hope to work with you more in the future." Before I can even acknowledge the compliment, Mr. Ware turns on his heel and walks off.

A smile creases another officer's tan face at Mr. Ware's commendation. "About those criminals. We caught them both. Those names, however, are mere forgeries. They are not their true titles."

"Then what are their real names?" I question as the Jetson boys and I hop into the police car.

"Daniel Stockire is the one known as Karl, and Tommy Jacobsen is the other criminal."

"Oh," I say, a bit puzzled.

Investigations by Scout Williams: Book 1

"What about the bomb?" Grant chirps.

"Oh, it will be removed and dismantled immediately," the man says as we drive down the familiar dirt road that leads to town. "Thank you, kids, for eliminating this impossible threat."

Jefferson and Grant glance at me. "It was really all Scout," Jefferson says. "She shut the whole bomb system down."

"But—" I try to explain what Jefferson and Grant did for me. But they will have nothing of it. I blush as the police guy praises me for my bravado and efficiency and all that stuff. (I don't understand half of the words he uses.) We pull up to the police station and enter the building. Two police hold Karl and JimBob, who are handcuffed. Karl gives me the dirtiest look I have ever received. I just smile uneasily and glance away. "Why did you want to blow us up?" I ask Daniel, aka Karl. Mr. Ware, amused and a little surprised, lets me do the questioning.

Daniel looks away dramatically as if owning up to his crime is the hardest thing ever. "Someone promised us big bucks if we blew up the dam."

"Who?" asks a policeman.

Daniel glances at JimBob, (Tommy), who shakes his head sadly.

"Guy in California, where I used to live. Name's Randy Callahan." Suddenly cooperative, Tommy lists a bunch of other info.

"Why didn't you just make a remote that would blow up the dam immediately instead of waiting five minutes? You could've done it once you were out of town." I wonder.

Investigations by Scout Williams: Book 1

Tommy shuffles his feet then glances at Daniel. "Well we wanted the thing to blow up no matter what. We didn't want the cops to catch us and take the remote if we made one."

"And why did you set up a cancel button?" I press.

"Cancel button?" JimBob, (Tommy), glances puzzledly at his companion.

Daniel, (Karl), shrugs carelessly.

Tommy rolls his eyes. "Oh, I know. It was that kid who rigged it up."

"What kid?" I press. "Washington Jetson?"

They nod vigorously, eager to shift the blame from themselves to Washington. "He and his brother."

"What?" Jefferson and Grant interject.

"How'd you know when we were down at The Court?" I press them even more.

"This other kid, Wash's brother or somethin'. Uhhhhh...What's his name, Dan?"

"Lincoln Jetson," I finish for him. I knew he was guilty.

Jefferson and Grant's faces drop. Grant looks stunned enough to cry, and Jefferson stutters, "Lincoln and Washington would...never do that!"

The nice officer pats their shoulders sympathetically. "Sorry, boys," he says. The two plop into waiting chairs simultaneously.

Investigations by Scout Williams: Book 1

Feeling even angrier at the baddies for luring my neighbors into being partners in crime, I ask another question. "Which of you wrote the note and latched it onto my brother's car?"

"Um, me," Daniel says, sighing as he stares at the ceiling.

Pursing my lips, I bombard them with more inquiries until they own up to every disgusting little secret, including bribing Vienna Daley and Washington into stealing the Chick-fil-A cash. Daniel admits that he called Mr. Johnson from Walt's flip-phone after he and JimBob kidnapped Walt.

They also confess that they kidnapped us because we were too nosy. Tommy explains that Washington and Lincoln had requested their little brothers to be abducted so they wouldn't be in the way of their 'money-making bomb-building-business.' They thought they would sell the bombs to mass weapon dealers for a little extra income. How sad for poor Jefferson and Grant.

Turns out the villains kidnapped Walt because he accidentally trudged by their secret hideout. Daniel and Tommy tracked Walt to The Court and threw him in their scary van and hauled him away.

CHAPTER 33 *Justice*

As the interrogation continues, a dog's bark comes from outside. The Jetson boys don't seem to notice it, as they're too sad, but I do. A woman screams. Mr. Ware, who's scrutinizing everyone in the room, raises an eyebrow and glances at Cal, the local sheriff. Cal and another policeman, holding yellow legal pads in their hands, glance at each other. The crooks look like they are glad for the averted attention. The officers set down their notebooks and hurry outside. I follow.

On the sidewalk across the street, a lady scrambles around, a dog up to her waist nipping at her. The lady, who's probably in her sixties, screams shrilly. The dog barks. "What's the meaning of this?" Sheriff Cal asks, rushing up to the woman.

"I left my glasses in the restaurant, and I went to get them. This dog, however, started to chase me. This dog," says the lady, quivering in anger. "Is biting me! Biting me, officer!"

"Well Mrs. Koates." Cal tries to keep from laughing. "This little puppy wasn't biting you. It was simply being playful."

Investigations by Scout Williams: Book 1

"Playful, Sheriff? Playful? Why, this puppy, as you call it, drew blood, Sheriff. Blood!"

I approach at this time. A German Shepard puppy sits by the two police, it's tongue lolling out. It looks up at me, curious.

Mrs. Koates continues to rave. "This is not a puppy! It's a dog! It's as tall as my chest, Sheriff!"

"Well Mrs. Koates, it is actually up to your waist."

"Not when it's sitting!" she shouts, looking down her nose at the puppy. "I declare it should be put down! A dog that bites must be put down. That was my father's rule. And my father was a sheriff!"

"Well Mrs. Koates, we can take this dog to the animal control, but we can't just put it down for being playful!"

"Oh yes you can," Mrs. Koates thrusts out her chin. "Do it, Sheriff. You know you should."

Sheriff Cal sighs agitatedly. "We'll take it to the animal control and ask them what's best. Jerry, go get the truck."

"Alright," Jerry, the other cop says, taking a wishful look at the German Shepard. "He *would* make a good police dog…"

"The animal control will say to put it down. I know it," Mrs. Koates harrumphs triumphantly, like she has foreseen the outcome of the situation.

At this point, the cute dog, still staring up at me with his placid, friendly brown eyes, starts to whine. He knows I want him. "Wait," I shout. "I'll take the dog."

Investigations by Scout Williams: Book 1

Jerry, the policeman who's walking off to get "the truck," turns around and stops. Cal smiles. Mrs. Koates looks me up and down with disapproval. "And who are you, a hillbilly?"

"Well Mrs. Koates," Cal interjects. "This is Scout Williams. She just saved our town from terrorists."

The old lady rolls her eyes. "Scout. What are they naming girls these days?" She storms off, having lost the battle.

"Can I have the dog? Please?" I plead. "You won't take him to Animal Control?"

"You can have him, Scout. He's a stray anyway. It's a shame. He'd make a good police dog."

"Don't worry officer," I smile, hugging the big puppy around the neck. "Police dog or not, Justice will always find a way to fight crime."

"Justice?" The sheriff cocks his head, amused.

"That's his name." I smile down at my new dog.

"Would you mind if I asked why?"

"I've always wanted justice. Now I know that God is the only One who can distribute it perfectly. He decides to be merciful and wait for all He has chosen to come to Him. Justice here will always remind me of that."

"Very good, young lady. Very good."

Investigations by Scout Williams: Book 1

CHAPTER 34   *Back Together*

The Jetson boys gape at Justice when I bring him in. I beam at them. Grant takes to stroking the dog to make himself feel better about the whole situation. Jefferson studies me for a moment, his elbows on his knees and his hands clasped in front of him. "He fits you," he states.

"What?"

"Your dog, Justice. He fits you."

I smile. "Now I just gotta convince Mom and Dad."

He grins fondly. "After what you just did, they'll let you have him."

Suddenly, the door whooshes open, and before I can breathe, Mom has me engulfed in a big hug. She doesn't even notice Justice. I laugh until I see what's happening with the Jetsons.

Mrs. Jetson holds her boys tight, but Jefferson and Grant just stare at Lincoln and Washington, who stare at the floor. "What?" Mrs. Jetson says, smiling. "What's the matter?" Then she

Investigations by Scout Williams: Book 1

looks up and sees Lincoln and Washington with handcuffs on. They had ridden with their mother, not knowing they had been found out.

"I'm...I'm so sorry, Mom," Lincoln shakes and his chin quivers.

"They offered me so much money!" Washington makes excuses.

Lincoln looks at me pleadingly. "Please, Scout, I'm sorry. I really am."

"Did you write that note, Lincoln? The one with a 'J?'" I question.

"No! I told you!"

You sure did! I scoff to myself.

"I wrote the note," Washington speaks up.

"Why?" I ask.

"Well you see," explains Washington. "I didn't want to use my computer because Mom and Dad always check what I do on it." He casts a scornful look at Mrs. Jetson. "So I wrote the note and tied it to a bush. I guess Karl never came and picked it up."

"Well we found it in the grass," I muse. "The wind must have blown it off. And the apple core?" I interrogate.

Washington slaps his forehead. "I forgot about that. I guess I threw it a little too close to the path." He sighs despondently.

"And your car, Lincoln," I continue. "The blue one. You were following us, weren't you."

Investigations by Scout Williams: Book 1

Lincoln looks pained. "Yes, Scout, I'm so sorry! I was just so worried you'd find our headquarters by Falcon Lake. That's why..." A tear rolls down his freckled face. "That's why I yelled at you on the phone the other day."

"And Mom," Lincoln adds. Washington gives him a shove. "We were going to go to Chicago next week to make more money. I'm sorry Mom. I'm so sorry. Washington is just so good at making bombs and I'm good at setting them in discreet places that I had to do it. They were offering us so much in the end. I was going to get 10,000 dollars, Mom. 10,000!"

Mrs. Jetson stares at Lincoln and Washington with her mouth slightly open, confused. Then she just breaks down into gushes of tears and ushers Jefferson and Grant out of the police station. She shuts the door softly.

Mom looks down, thanks Sheriff Cal who is calling Vienna to jail and glares at Daniel and Tommy who hang their heads ashamedly. Before we walk out through the dark night to the car, I notice with a surge of fear that Mom and Daniel's eyes meet, Daniel scowling at her with so much hatred that I'm worried for my mother's life. Does she know this man? Mr. Ware notices the interaction too, and he stares at me accusingly like I'm supposed to know what's going on between them.

Finally, Mom sees Justice following me. "Go home, boy," she waves him away. "Go home."

The dog clamps his jaw shut and cocks his big head. His ears swivel up. Justice glances at me questioningly.

"He's my dog, Mom," I explain, nervous of what she might say. "The police let me have him."

Investigations by Scout Williams: Book 1

Mom watches Justice jump into the backseat, amazed at the German Shepard's size. "We'll see," she shakes her head. "We'll see what your father says."

While we're driving home, it suddenly clicks that my friend Jennifer had been uptight about the mystery on the last day of school because she knew her sister was involved. I hope Jenn isn't convicted or anything like that. "I'm so glad you're safe," Mom says, choked-up. "I don't know what I'd do if..." Mom stops there, covering her trembling lips with a hand.

"Mom, why was Daniel scowling at you like that?"

"Scowling at me? Like what?" Mom suddenly gets overly curious. So curious that I know she knows exactly why Daniel Stockire was scowling at her.

"Well," I reply. "He had the nastiest look on his face." I try to hide that I know that she knows.

Mom glances at me. I'm worried that she knows that I know that she knows that I know. She clenches her jaw. "You must've imagined it." Then she changes the subject abruptly. "Smith feels pretty bad about what happened..." Mom trails off. "So, don't be too hard on him." Then she prattles on about how I need to be more careful, how adults should assist children in dangerous situations, etc., etc.

When we finally arrive home, Smith adores Justice and has me tell him the whole story twice before he lets me go to bed.

I slide under the covers of my bed and sit against the pillows, Justice dozing off on the floor. God sure has worked this out. God...Usually, I would've given myself the credit. Usually...But I've changed through this adventure. Changed a lot. When I was

Investigations by Scout Williams: Book 1

little, God was a given. My parents took me to church, and I prayed all the time. A few days ago, I didn't even know who I was praying to. I wasn't a real a Christian. I realize I never have been.

I know that my sin separates me from the Almighty God. The justice that He has every right to act upon is withheld from me because His Son died in my place and received the punishment that I should receive. I deserve eternal punishment: hell. I know I'm not worthy of God's salvation. No human being is. A verse rings in my head, whispering, *'All have sinned and fall short of the glory of God.' Romans 3:23.*

I didn't realize—or maybe I just didn't care—that it was the Creator of the universe who saved me. I am His enemy. I can't imagine a holy God saving His sworn enemy, me, from something as terrible as the punishment for sin, which is death and hell. A God who died a horrible death on a cross to save me—me!—from all my wrongdoings and bad thoughts and things I don't even realize is sin. Who willingly died and suffered for me. Who rose again on the third day and defeated death to rescue me. Who offers me new life. Eternal life. A purposeful life that I can live for His glory. A God who offers to save every human being from this plight.

My faith has been stale. In fact, it's never been there at all. And I need to do something about it. God protected me when I tried to protect someone else, so He deserves the glory for everything I do.

And so, I pray for His forgiveness. I ask Jesus Christ into my heart. I thank Him for His justice. I pray that He will help me long for justice just like Him.

Investigations by Scout Williams: Book 1

The next morning, as I mess with my organic flavorless rice-puff cereal, the doorbell rings. Justice bays his deep, throaty bark. Mom answers the door and calls, "Scout! Guests for you!"

I stand up, glad to leave my cereal to get soggy so I won't have to eat it and skip to the door. It's the Jetsons, excluding Lincoln and Washington, but including their dad. "Scout," he says in a deep voice. "I'd like to thank you for rescuing these two rascals." He gives Jefferson and Grant a look.

"Thanks," Jefferson says, scuffing the toe of his sneaker on the 'Welcome All' rug. He's suddenly very shy.

"Yeah," Grant echoes. "Thanks."

"Won't you come in?" Mom invites Mr. and Mrs. Jetson. "Roger's just in his room." She calls to my dad.

I step onto the porch with Jefferson and Grant. "So..." Jefferson studies the doormat. "Want to play basketball?"

"Sure," I smile and say exactly what I said the other day. "Although I'm not that good at it."

Investigations by Scout Williams: Book 1

CHAPTER 35   *Basketball Again*

We play basketball all day. When the sun starts to set, Jefferson teaches me how to shoot a basic trick shot.

"Here," Jefferson gently takes the ball from me. "Let me show you. *That's* not the way you shoot a fade-away."

He demonstrates the shot perfectly.

"Wow," I say.

Grant walks up with his ball. "I can do a fade-away too!"

"Let's see it," his brother challenges.

Grant misses horribly but his form is good.

"You know," Jefferson sets his hands on his hips and watches Grant's ball bounce away. "You *are* pretty good at basketball, Scout. You said you weren't."

I shrug.

Investigations by Scout Williams: Book 1

Just then, Justice comes bounding from my back porch. He jumps on Grant, and the dog is taller than the boy when he stands on his hind legs. "Get your giant dog off of me!" he shouts.

I laugh and pull Justice off of Grant by his new leather collar. Then, contentedly, we all sit down on the warm concrete at the same time.

"What's one thing you learned, Scout," Jefferson muses. He leans back on his hands and watches the sun set.

"What?"

"One thing you learned during the kidnapping."

"I learned that God is just. But He's just in a loving way. He desires all men to know Him. I'm just glad He chose me." I hug my knees to myself.

"And me," says Jefferson.

"And me," says Grant.

"What did you learn, Grant?" Jefferson turns to his brother.

"God protects His people." Grant's answer is surprisingly profound.

"That's right," I agree, stroking Justice. "And even if you're not yet His child, God uses pain and doubt to bring you to Himself."

"I learned that you can't trust a soul in this world," Jefferson states with a sigh, staring off into space. "Not even your own brothers."

"That's not true!" disagrees Grant. "You can trust me!"

Investigations by Scout Williams: Book 1

Jefferson smiles at the sunset.

"And me," I smile. "But most importantly, you can trust the loving God of justice that washed away our sin. My goal is to share that with everyone I meet."

Investigations by Scout Williams: Book 1

Epilogue

About two weeks after my kidnapping, Smith, Mom, Dad, and I sit on the back porch. Mom is watering her dear flowers, Dad is engrossed in the newspaper, Smith is looking up ways to effectively clean your car on his phone, and I'm reading a mystery novel with Justice at my feet. Thankfully, Dad let me keep him. Mostly, though, my dog hangs outside since his constant shedding gets on Mom's nerves.

All of a sudden Mom looks at Dad and Dad looks at Smith and Smith looks at me. I raise an eyebrow questionably. "Well," Dad starts, flapping his newspaper over the arm of his chair as Mom plops into a yard seat next to Dad. "Your mother has something to say."

"Kids," Mom starts. She looks nervous. "I believe our family's in danger."

Investigations by Scout Williams: Book 1

Acknowledgements

Thank you to my editorial committee: Chloe P., Dasha K., Annie G., and of course Mom and Dad. Also, many thanks to my siblings letting me read this aloud to them and always being ready to listen and help.

I also am greatly in debt to Mom, the best writing teacher the world has ever seen, and Mrs. Johnson, my writing coach, for assisting me in my world of words.

Also, thanks to my cousins Zoe and Lily. Zoe, for spreading the word around that *Justice* is out, and Lily, for telling me the truth no matter how blunt it is.

And lastly, I thank God for using me and my writing as a tool to get His message out to the world.

Looking to see more cases that Scout Williams will crack? Don't miss *Investigations by Scout Williams: Trust*, which is coming soon.

Thank you for reading *Justice* by Freedom Fairway.

Made in the USA
Monee, IL
04 August 2020